Remedy of the Witch

Crypt Witch cozy paranormal mystery series - book 10

K.E. O'Connor

K.E. O'Connor Books

REMEDY OF THE WITCH

Copyright © 2022 by K.E. O'Connor

ISBN: 978-1-915378-08-8

Written by: K.E. O'Connor

Chapter 1

I stuffed the plump, lavender scented pillow over my head to drown out the bickering that had been raging for five minutes.

"She's always liked me better than you," Bandit said. "That's why Tempest brought me here and left your chunky behind in Willow Tree Falls."

"That's not true," Wiggles said on the other end of the snow globe. "You know I can't leave the village."

"That's an excuse," Bandit said. "If Tempest wanted you in Puzzlewood, you'd be here."

I groaned and hurled the pillow at Bandit. "Quit teasing my hellhound. He's right. He can't leave Willow Tree Falls."

Bandit sat on the edge of her bed in the motel room we were using as our temporary base, a gleeful look on her sparkly face. "A fairy never lies. I'm here because you like me the best."

"Tempest, tell me that's not true." A note of anxiety threaded through Wiggles' words as his nose loomed large in the snow globe.

"I'm insulted you even have to ask that question," I said. "You know I'd have brought you with me if I could."

Since we'd arrived in Puzzlewood on the hunt for my dad less than twenty-four hours ago, Wiggles had been messaging at every opportunity.

Not that I minded him getting in touch. It was sweet that he missed me. But it was inconvenient, especially when I needed to be laser-focused on tracking down Dad and not worrying about what was going on back home.

The thought of finding my dad sent a shiver of anticipation through me. I hadn't seen him for years. It felt like I was on the cusp of something momentous that would affect the whole family. Our lives were about to change if this worked out.

"I hope you're looking after Tempest properly," Wiggles said.

"I can look after myself just fine." I slid off the silky comforter on my deluxe bed and walked over to the table.

We'd checked into what I'd figured was a basic motel, but I'd been surprised by the luxury. And the staff had bent over backward to accommodate us. They hadn't blinked an eye at the enormous fairy accompanying me, who shed glitter wherever she went.

"Aurora wanted me to ask if you're eating properly," Wiggles said.

"We left the village a day ago. I can't have become malnourished in that short amount of time."

Wiggles sniffed. "You must at least be hungry."

I shrugged. "I could definitely eat." My fingers traced over the hard wood table that was set with a platter of treats.

I'd forgotten how great Puzzlewood was. We used to vacation here years ago. Back then, I'd seen it through a child's eyes, all the fun things to do and the great tasting food to stuff down, but this place had some seriously amazing luxury for the adults too.

I plucked a complimentary chocolate off the table and popped it into my mouth.

"Hey! What are you eating?" Wiggles asked.

"Only the finest chocolate you're never going to taste," Bandit said. "And we're not bringing any back for you if you keep pestering us."

"Of course, we are." I turned to the snow globe. "How's everything back home?"

Wiggles' red eyes glowed for a second as I chewed the chocolate. "Granny Dottie and Aurora haven't worked up the courage to tell your mom what's going on."

I blew out a breath, an unwelcome throb of tension in my shoulders. I was glad I'd left them to break the news to the rest of the family about this mission. It wasn't the bravest move on my part, but Mom would have panicked, flapped around, and then insisted she come with me.

I needed to check things out before anyone else got involved. Dad had been gone a long time, and as much as I tried to fool myself, he'd be a different man from the one I remembered.

"Make sure you prod them into action before too long," I said. "And don't let Granny Dottie anywhere near the brandy before she's revealed what's going on. She needs a clear head when this news comes out."

"It's too late for that," Wiggles said. "She was sneaking the stuff into her morning oatmeal. What are you going to do now you're there?"

I wrinkled my nose. "Take a look around. See if anyone's seen Dad. Get his picture out there. Maybe he'll hear that we're looking for him and come find us."

"And then we're going to enjoy the facilities at Puzzlewood," Bandit said. "They have a water park. No one told me about that. I'd have brought my rubber ring."

"We're not here for fun," I said. "This isn't a vacation. Let's not get distracted." I pushed aside the brochure about the water park Bandit offered me.

"One tiny hour enjoying ourselves won't hurt anyone," Bandit said. "It'll be fun."

"You can't go to the water park with her," Wiggles said, a growl echoing through the snow globe and making it rattle.

"She can hardly take you," Bandit said. "You'd shed fur everywhere and make the water smell like rotten eggs with your sulfuric stink."

"I could wear a onesie bathing costume," Wiggles said. "It would be fine. Don't go to the water park with Bandit."

"No one's going to any water park," I said. "Wiggles, you concentrate on keeping the family together. Once word about this gets out, they'll be tricky to deal with."

"Of course. I won't let you down," he said.

"I'm bored. And we need to get more food," Bandit said. "Flying always makes me hungry. And I was carrying extra weight."

Bandit had flown us to Puzzlewood in record time. My stomach still wasn't settled from the bumpy journey, but it had been a quick way to get here. Plus, I'd been concentrating so hard on not being ill that I'd not had time to worry that I was about to find my dad after all this time.

"Stick to salads and plain food," Wiggles said. "Don't go eating pizza together. Pizza is our food. Tempest, promise me you won't eat pizza with that sparkling beast."

Poor Wiggles. He hated that he wasn't with me. And I didn't like leaving him behind. But thanks to the magic I'd used to bring him back to life as a hellhound, he could never leave Willow Tree Falls. That left me stuck with one enormous, mildly deranged fairy as a sidekick. I still wasn't certain it was a great idea that Bandit was here with me.

"We'd better go," I said.

"Make sure you check in with me every hour," Wiggles said.

"I'll try for once a day. Take care of everyone back there." We said our goodbyes. I ended the connection and placed the snow globe back on the bedside table.

"So, food and then the water park?" Bandit stood and stretched her enormous wings, flapping them around and causing a small hurricane in the room.

"No! This place is big, and we've only been around a fraction of it since we arrived. We need to get the word out that we're looking for my dad."

"We still need to eat," Bandit said. "Those chocolates are great, but I need my fruits and veggies. I'll be five minutes. I'll go get some chips and dip for you and something yummy for me." She turned to the window and grunted. "I thought this place always had perfect weather."

"It does. It's one of the things people love about it. You can always guarantee sunshine."

"Not today, you can't." She strode to the window.

I joined her and stared at the huge hailstones that hammered down outside. "That's weird."

"Hail doesn't bother me," Bandit said. "I'll go grab the food."

Before I had a chance to protest that we were wasting time, she flung the door open and shot into the sky.

I slammed it shut to stop the hail from getting in and continued to stare out the window. People raced past, their hands covering their heads as they tried to dodge the hailstones that rained down on them. The hail was big enough to chip glass. There must be something off with the weather magic in Puzzlewood.

I stepped away from the window and turned to the mirror. I looked paler than usual, most likely due to my bad night of sleep yesterday. I smoothed my hands down my hair. What would Dad think of me after all this time? Would he even recognize me? I was about a foot taller and had filled out my gawky teenage frame, but other than that, I didn't look much different.

He couldn't have forgotten about us. He must have stayed away because it was best for the whole family. He'd always been a selfless guy, putting the family first. That had to be the reason he'd walked out.

I was certain that, once I found him, everything would be explained, and he'd be happy to come back to Willow Tree Falls. Back to the family he belonged in.

I patted my chest. "What do you think, Frank? Are you happy that I'm about to find my dad after all these years?"

My incumbent demon, Frank, had been refusing to communicate for months. I was worried that his lack of communication was connected to my dad's disappearance. Rumor had it that a deal had been made between Frank and my dad that involved him having to leave the village.

I couldn't believe that, but if Dad thought it was best for me and would keep the family safe, I bet he'd make any deal that was needed. Even with a sly, deceitful demon who loved to cause chaos.

Frank, as had become the norm, remained silent on the matter.

"I'll get the truth out of you soon enough," I said. "You're living on borrowed time."

The door swung open. Bandit swooped in with a bag of groceries and a large white box in her hands. "Brunch is served." She set everything down with a flourish.

I unpacked the food. There was an enormous bowl of salad for Bandit, six bags of chips, a range of dips, prepacked sandwiches and cakes, and inside the white box, a tray of chocolate brownies.

"This will keep us going the whole time we're here," I said.

"Not the way I eat, it won't." Bandit scooped up the salad in her hand and began to eat. "You're only allowed one brownie."

"How generous." I eyed the dozen chocolate chip brownies that tempted me to skip the rest of the food and dive straight into the dessert.

"I'm just giving you a friendly warning," Bandit said. "You take more than one, and I'll break your hand."

I glowered at her. She would as well. Bandit was ten times stronger than me, and her glitter came with a stinging side-effect. I was just grateful that she was indebted to Aurora for taking her in when she'd been turned into a cat. Otherwise, we wouldn't be friends.

We set to work on the food, and I settled back on my bed with my solitary brownie by my side and a large bag of cheesy chips and garlic dip.

Bandit stuffed down the salad in a couple of minutes and grabbed two brownies. "I've been meaning to talk to you about something."

"What's that?"

She stretched out a wing and examined it. "It's about your dad."

I leaned forward on the bed. "Did you see him when you went out?"

"Oh, no, nothing like that." Bandit glanced away. "It's about the message I was supposed to give you."

"I already know about the message. Dad sent you to Willow Tree Falls to let us know he was safe."

"You're exactly right." Bandit bobbled her head from side to side.

"And yet there's something you missed?"

"It's a minor thing. I may have been a bit tardy about passing on the message."

"How tardy are we talking?" Bandit had only shown up in Willow Tree Falls a few months ago.

"About ten years."

My brownie fell from my hand. "You were supposed to tell us that Dad was alive and safe as soon as he left Willow Tree Falls?"

"Correct. We met three weeks after he left. We got talking, and he asked for my help."

"What the heck were you doing all that time?"

"I got distracted. It's easy to do. This world is a fascinating place. Your dad gave me the message and told me where to find you. He paid me well, so I was happy to do it."

"You got... distracted?" My fingers flexed, and magic sparked out of them.

"There's no point in getting your panties in a knot," Bandit said. "I got to you in the end."

"After you fooled around for a decade, got turned into a cat, and forgot the message you were supposed to tell us."

"Eventually, I remembered what I was supposed to do," Bandit said. "I did an excellent job. And being a cat is a traumatic experience. The less important things had to take a back seat."

I jumped off the bed and stalked toward her. "We spent years wondering where Dad was. We didn't know if he was dead or alive." I jabbed a finger against her chest. "And all this time, you knew.

You had a message and didn't bother to pass it on because you got side-tracked."

Bandit's wings fluttered around her. "You have to remember, fairies live for thousands of years. For me, a decade is a blink of the eye."

"Not for us. It was a horrible time for the family. It could have been avoided if you'd passed on the message when you were supposed to. Even if we hadn't been able to find him, for whatever reason, we'd have known he was okay."

"You're stressing about nothing. Besides, witches live a long time too," Bandit said. "And you know now, so everything is sorted."

"Everything is not sorted." Bandit had to be kidding if she thought she could get away with this.

"It's as good as. We're here. Your dad is almost within touching distance. No harm was done."

Occasionally, there were times when I wished I had access to Frank's demon power. I'd have loved nothing more than to slam this fairy into the ground. But she had vicious wings, killer glitter, and teeth that could shred metal. Still, the urge to punch her was rearing up.

However, I had one weapon I could use against her. One that she'd do anything to avoid. It may be petty, but I was angry.

"I'm telling Aurora about this."

"Oh! You don't need to trouble her." Worry flickered across Bandit's face. She had a serious gooey spot for my little sister.

I shook my head and made sure to look sad. "Aurora cares about you. She took you in when no one else was interested in you. She nursed you back to health when you got sick, and all this time, you were hiding an important bit of information from her. She won't be so fond of you when she finds out about this."

Bandit scooped a wing around me and crushed me to her chest. "There's no need to involve Aurora. I'm telling you now because, when we meet your dad, he may remember what happened between us. I don't want any secrets."

"I hope he remembers. I'm hoping he's as angry as I am." I struggled in the tight embrace she held me in. It felt like a steel vice had wrapped around me.

"I'm helping now." Bandit shuffled me closer. "Aurora doesn't need to know about this. I'm sorry if it caused you any inconvenience."

"Inconvenience!" I thumped her chest and sparked hot magic against her skin until she released me. "Wiggles is right. Fairies can never be trusted."

Her nostrils flared. "I'm trustworthy. As soon as I finish these brownies, we'll find your dad and make everything right. You'll be so happy to see him that you'll forget my tiny oversight."

I glared at her. "Don't count on it."

"Maybe another brownie will change your mind." Bandit held out a dark chocolate brownie.

"I thought you'd break my hand if I had more than one."

"This is a peace offering. You may have two, but no more, or the hand breaking promise comes into play."

"Keep it." I was so angry with her that I'd lost my appetite. Even the alluring brownies no longer held any appeal.

I had to focus on finding my dad. I'd deal with this deceitful fairy another time.

Chapter 2

The weather spell was still malfunctioning when we left the motel and headed into the center of Puzzlewood. There was a chill wind, and rain threatened as we walked past the rows of cute hobbit-like cottages and entered the main shopping parade.

Puzzlewood was set out on a grid system. In the four corners sat the accommodation for visitors, with a large water park at one end and an amusement park with death-defying rides at the other. In the center sat an enormous mall full of restaurants, cafes, and all the shopping opportunities you could ever dream of.

Ringing Puzzlewood was a huge forest that offered hiking, biking, and even abseiling if you were the outdoorsy type.

"Where do you want to focus the search?" Bandit strolled along beside me.

"We need to ask everywhere and everyone," I said. "Let's start in the stores and work our way through them. Most people will be inside since the weather's so grim."

"Are you sure you don't want to start at the water park?" Bandit asked. "Maybe your dad works there. If I had to get a job, I'd definitely submit my resume to that place. Imagine getting paid to go on the rides every day."

"That's not what you do if you work at a water park. You get to clean up after the tourists, usually the mess over-excited children leave behind when they've had too much to eat and been shaken around for an hour on loads of fast moving rides."

"Hmm, that doesn't sound like so much fun."

"No, it's not, so we're not starting there. Let's move before those clouds dump their load on our heads."

Bandit grumbled under her breath but followed along behind me.

We entered the ground floor of the mall, and I suppressed a groan as I saw there were over two hundred stores and restaurants to make our way through. This would take some time. Still, that's what we were here for.

I pulled my shoulders back and entered the candy store. The scent of warm sugar blended with tangy lemon, vanilla, and cinnamon made my mouth water.

There were several customers browsing the rows of candies, and two squat, smiley brownies were behind the counter, dressed in sage green uniforms.

I waited until they were free then walked over with the picture of my dad. "Have you seen this man?"

The brownie stacking a pile of sherbet lemons paused. She took the picture and studied it before handing it to her colleague. "Sorry, my love, he's not familiar. Has he gone missing?"

"He has," I said. "A long time ago. He's called Artie Crypt. He'll be ten years older than that picture, but he won't look much different." At least, I hoped he wouldn't. How much could a person physically change in a decade?

"He must not have a sweet tooth," the brownie's colleague said as she passed back the photo. "We're the most popular candy store in Puzzlewood. We've been open for fifty years and know all of our regular customers. We'll keep an eye out for him, though."

Bandit walked over, her arms piled high with candied apples. She had several stuffed in her mouth.

The shop assistants glanced at each other. "Is that our whole stock of candied apples you've got there?"

"I'll take any more if you've got them out back." Bandit's words were barely distinguishable as she chewed. "These are incredible. They taste even better than the real thing. And they're apple-shaped, so they fit my diet."

I shook my head. "Pay for those and let's get out of here."

"Pay?" Bandit glanced at me. "I don't carry money on me."

I sighed as I pulled out my wallet and handed money to one of the assistants. "Thanks for your help." I ushered Bandit out of the store before she snaffled more treats I'd have to pay for.

We tried the next five stores and got the same response. No one recognized my dad from the photo I had of him.

I turned around to leave the stationery store and couldn't see Bandit. I walked around the store, but there was no sign of her. How much trouble could she get in in a place selling notepads and fancy pens?

I headed out of the store and spotted her large green frame slinking out the main doors of the mall. What was she up to?

I raced after her. "Hold it right there."

Bandit turned and grinned. "What? I'm not doing anything wrong."

"You're skulking. Where are you going?"

"Who says I'm going anywhere?"

"Me."

She sighed and looked over her shoulder. "You don't need me. You're doing fine on your own. I figured I'd check things out at the water park."

"Stay here," I said. "I may need you as backup. That's the whole point of Aurora insisting you come with me."

"Just half an hour at the water park. That's all I need," Bandit said. "I have trouble concentrating if I don't get what I want."

"No kidding," I said. "But as I've already said, we're not here to have fun."

"Surely we can have a little fun," Bandit said. "And I'm certain we'll find your dad at the water park."

I moved closer. "Why? Is that another part of the message you forgot to pass on?"

"No, but it makes sense. Everyone who lives in this place must want to hang out at the water park. You get to have fun all day."

"We'll get around to the water park," I said.

"You need to lighten up. Come on." Bandit grabbed hold of me and leaped into the air.

It felt like I'd left my stomach on the ground as we shot above the rooftops. "Put me down."

"You'll love it when we get there," Bandit said. "I've read the brochure. They have the dragon's revenge ride, zip coasters, giant slides, aqua loops, waterfalls, and surfing rides."

"No. Water. Park." I squirmed in her grip as she gained height.

"Yes, water park," Bandit said. "I can't wait to tell Wiggles all about this. He'll be furious."

"You're only doing this to make him jealous," I said.

"Do you think it'll work?"

"No! Now, put me down."

"Are you sure about that?"

"Yes. We need to get back to the stores and keep asking around about Dad. We don't have time for this."

"Okay. You're the boss." Bandit released her hold on me.

I yelped and flailed my arms. She had not just dropped me mid-flight? I tried to grab hold of something but came up with air. I flipped around, and my eyes widened. Oh, crud. There was an enormous pool below me full of swimmers.

My arms shot out, and I conjured a slowdown spell. It was just enough to stop me from slamming into the water at fifty miles an hour as I hit the surface and went under.

When I resurfaced, a lifeguard was blasting a whistle at me and jabbing his finger. "No dive bombing."

I raised a hand as I sucked in a breath. If only he'd seen just how far I'd dived from.

"And no swimming fully clothed," the lifeguard said. "Get out of the pool."

I swam to the side and hauled myself out, trying not to notice the unhappy glares from parents, who were keeping their children out of my way.

A second later, Bandit appeared by my side. "Nice dive. Wasn't that incredible?"

I pulled myself to my feet, water dripping off me. "I'm going to kill you."

"Now, now. I was trying to get you to see how much fun this place is. We can search for your dad *and* enjoy ourselves. Everyone's a winner." Bandit beamed at me as if this was the most brilliant idea she'd ever had.

"I am done with you," I said. "You're not here to help; you're here to cause chaos. Are you even on my side?"

"Um, well, I guess."

"You guess?"

"I'm on Aurora's side, so by default, I'm on your side."

"It doesn't feel like it right now." My feet squelched in my boots as a lightning bolt spell flickered from my fingers, and a rod of crackling energy appeared.

Bandit raised her hand, an amused glint in her eyes. "Calm down. I didn't realize you wouldn't enjoy getting wet."

"What I don't enjoy is being yanked around like I'm your pet. Did you even know there was a pool below us before you dropped me?"

"I figured there was a fifty-fifty chance there'd be water. After all, this is a water park."

Letting out a cry of rage, I thrust the lightning bolt at Bandit.

She shielded herself with her wings, and sparks of magic shot around her as the spell impacted.

She shook out her wing and glared at me. "That's not friendly. You've singed me."

"I'll do more than singe you."

The lifeguard hurried over, his cheeks bright red and matching his skimpy shorts. "No dangerous magic in the water park." He pointed at the board of rules on the wall. "No dive bombing, no eating in the pool, no heavy petting, no dangerous magic. There are families here. People come here for a good time. They don't want to see fights."

I glanced at him. He couldn't be more than eighteen, and his eyes were full of fear. I had to admire his bravery. Bandit could snap him in two if she had a mind to.

"I'll have to ask you to leave," the lifeguard said.

"Not yet. I haven't been on a single ride," Bandit said. "I hear the Dragon's Revenge is amazing."

"You're both banned from the water park," the lifeguard said.

Bandit huffed, and her wings fluttered out. "That's not fair. Tempest threw magic at me. I was protecting myself. I'm innocent."

"You're far from innocent. And it's more than fair after what you did to me," I said. "Let's get out of here before we're banned from Puzzlewood." I stalked away, not caring if she followed. Bandit was a liability. I should never have agreed to bring her with me.

After a few seconds, she caught up with me. We walked along in a tense silence until we were out of the water park and heading back to the stores.

"I shouldn't have dropped you," Bandit said, a sullen note in her voice. "Don't tell Aurora what I did. I don't want her to be angry at me."

"Then start helping me," I said. "Help to get our dad back and she'll love you forever."

"She already loves me."

"Then she'll love you even more."

"More than the sap she's dating?"

"Lex! You're jealous of him?"

"He gets in the way when we're trying to have a night in. And I don't like the way he looks at Aurora."

I glanced at Bandit. "How does he look at her?"

"Like she's a prize heifer."

I choked out a laugh. "He doesn't." Aurora had pretty lousy taste in guys, but Lex Fontaine seemed like a good one. "Maybe if you quit misbehaving, Aurora may choose to spend her time with you rather than her boyfriend."

"You'll put in a good word for me? Make sure Aurora knows how amazing I've been."

"So long as you stop messing about."

"Of course. No more fun for me."

"Good."

"Here, let me dry you off."

I yelped as Bandit blasted me with a fire spell. I danced around, my hair singeing as I patted out the green and orange flames flickering around me.

"Enough with your crazy magic." I touched what was left of my eyebrows and growled at her. They'd take months to grow back.

"You're dry now," Bandit said. "You see, I'm helping."

"I'm char-grilled." I gritted my teeth. It seemed increasingly likely that one of us wasn't getting out of this place alive if she kept on like this. "Tell me again the exact words my dad used in the message he gave you."

"He simply said that he was fine. He had to leave Willow Tree Falls to keep everyone safe. He instructed me that I was to be your guardian and make sure no trouble came your way."

"You did a lousy job of that," I said.

"That's a touch unfair. And when I finally got to Willow Tree Falls, I was a cat. I did an amazing job as soon as I remembered my mission. I protected Aurora."

"You turned into a predatory, terrifying fairy who wanted to tear off everyone's head if they got within ten feet of my sister."

"Exactly. She seemed the most vulnerable at the time. I fulfilled my mission perfectly. And I bonded with Aurora. It was only right that I protected her the most."

"And the rest of the family weren't worth watching over? We'd have appreciated knowing about our dad as soon as he gave you that message."

Bandit scratched her nose with the tip of her wing. "I may be amazing, but I'm not perfect. I need more food." She stomped off, glitter cascading from her wings.

I slowed and shook my head. Great, now I had an angry, insane fairy to deal with. If she thought hurling me into a pool was a fun time, I'd hate to discover what she did to her enemies.

I turned in a slow circle, overwhelm punching my gut as I saw how big this place was. I needed to be more strategic, so I could get the word out about my dad quickly.

A shimmer of movement had my head turning. A tiny angel flitted toward me on shiny white wings. She looked like no angel I'd ever seen before. They were normally a solid six foot plus, but I couldn't mistake the shiny blonde hair and white uniform.

She stopped in front of my face and hovered, a smile on her pretty face. "Dazielle wishes to speak to you."

I tilted my head. What did the head of Angel Force back home want with me? "What are you, some kind of messenger angel?"

"Correct. You're to find the nearest snow globe and contact her. It's urgent."

Dazielle's idea of urgent and mine were often different. "Tell her I'll get in touch later today."

"No, you're to contact her immediately. I'm not to leave your side until you do so."

I didn't need another fluttering, winged interference in my life. So I headed into the nearest cafe, grabbed a coffee, and paid to use their snow globe before settling at a table by the window.

As soon as I activated a link to Dazielle on the snow globe, the tiny angel finger-waved me and vanished.

"Tempest, you got my message?" Dazielle appeared on the snow globe.

"This isn't a social call. I got it. What's up?"

"Someone's been murdered. And a demon is involved."

I shook my head. "Not my problem. You need to get somebody else on this case. I can't get involved."

"Yes, you can. You're in the perfect position to help."

"I don't see how. I'm nowhere near Willow Tree Falls."

"The murder took place in Puzzlewood. I know you're there. Aurora told me."

I took a sip of my coffee. What else had she been confiding to Dazielle? "I don't have time to go demon hunting for you."

"I'm also aware of why you're in Puzzlewood."

I raised my eyebrows. "Aurora told you that?"

"No, but your sister is terrible at hiding things. I simply put the pieces together from the pauses and gaps in her story. This is an easy job. I just want you to take a look. The demon is already in custody. I need someone to corroborate the witness statements and return the prisoner to me."

I leaned forward, my nose almost touching the snow globe. "No. I'm looking for my dad. I can't afford any distractions."

"This will take a couple of hours, tops. You'll get paid for an easy transport and release."

"If it's so easy, why don't you fly over and grab the demon?"

"I'm needed elsewhere." She let out a sigh. "And this wasn't a pleasant crime."

"When is murder ever pleasant?"

"I mean, this was messy," Dazielle said. "You're experienced in messy."

"If you're trying to soften me up with compliments, you're doing a terrible job."

"This demon almost destroyed the victim. Something nasty is in Puzzlewood. You're our expert demon catcher."

"Why can't the local angels deal with this demon?"

She shook her head. "This is Puzzlewood. The angels don't have much experience with dark energies. There hasn't been a murder there in eighty years. They'd appreciate your input."

"Just like you always appreciate my input when there's a mystery to solve." I arched a brow and took another sip of my coffee. Let her grovel a bit. Dazielle always gave me a hard time when I helped out with cases she struggled with.

Her lips pursed. "I'll admit you can sometimes be a nuisance, but you have your value. The angels there are very welcoming. They'll be glad to get the demon out of Puzzlewood as swiftly as possible. They don't allow any demons in there and don't want the reputation of the area damaged by this incident. This is a quick in and out job."

That didn't sound so bad, and the extra money would come in handy. "I'll take a look but no promises. And I'm not leaving here until I find my dad. I may have to put the demon on ice while I deal with my own business."

She nodded. "Of course. And how's that business going?"

"No luck yet, but we've not been here long. There are a lot of people to talk to."

"I hope you find what you're looking for," Dazielle said. "Give your dad my best when you locate him. I always had time for Artie. He was a good guy."

"Thanks. Will do." After getting details of the angels to contact, I ended the connection and sat back in my seat. My dad had been the best guy. But that was ten years ago. Would he still be so nice after a decade and a lot of history had passed?

Chapter 3

As tempting as it was to stamp my feet and tell anyone who'd listen that the world wasn't fair, I resisted the desire to revert into petulant teenager mode as I continued asking around about my dad.

I'd been asking the same question all afternoon and getting nowhere. Plus, Bandit had abandoned me. If I found out she'd slunk off to the water park for a day of fun, I'd be firing her glittery behind and telling Aurora what a lousy, sneaky fairy she was.

I stood outside the Creamy Dreams and Tasty Tarts Bakery, only half-aware of the tempting treats behind the glass in front of me, when something prodded my left cheek.

I turned and was met with another tiny angel fluttering her wings and smiling.

"Greetings, Tempest Crypt."

"Do you need something?" I asked, not in the mood for being pleasant.

"Dazielle wants to know why you haven't reported to the local branch of Angel Force to deal with the demon matter."

"Because I'm busy. Her case will have to wait." I walked to the next store.

The angel fluttered along with me. "It's important you report to the station. The angels only work a nine-to-five in Puzzlewood. They'll soon be closed."

I glanced at her. "What happens if a crime occurs when they're off duty?"

"It never does. The people in Puzzlewood are well-behaved. They come here for fun. not fighting."

I checked the time. If what she said was true, the angels would close their doors in less than an hour. "I'll drop by tomorrow."

"You need to go now." The angel prodded me on the cheek again.

I batted her away. "I'll get around to it when I've got spare time. Right now, I'm all out of that and have another ten stores to visit."

"You weren't doing anything when I arrived, other than staring at cake." The angel fluttered around my head, her tiny white feathers raining down on my black jacket.

I brushed them away and grimaced. Maybe I could do with a break. No one knew anything about my dad, and they didn't recognize him from the photograph I was showing around. The angels could even be useful in helping to locate him. He was technically a missing person.

"I'll report you to Dazielle if you don't complete your work task," the angel said, her voice growing squeaky.

"Report away. I don't work for Dazielle." I turned and stomped off.

I'd seen a brilliant white building in the center of Puzzlewood as I'd walked around. All Angel Force buildings looked the same. It was as if they got a new coat of shimmering white paint every day so they looked pristine.

The fluttering angel accompanied me until I reached the door of the Angel Force building, but I didn't acknowledge her. Hopefully, she'd go away once she saw I was following orders like a good little demon hunter.

I slowed as I walked through the doorway. Big bunches of flowers sat on tables next to comfy armchairs. Was I in the right place? A quick glance along the walls confirmed I was. These angels had the same motivational slogans across their walls as the branch in Willow Tree Falls. But this was on another level of warm and welcoming. There was even a big plate of cookies on the reception desk as I walked toward it. Wiggles would have been in his element in this place.

"Welcome to Angel Force." A stunning blonde angel smiled at me from behind the desk. "I hope you're having a glorious day. How may I assist you?"

"Um, it's not been great so far. I'm here about the murder."

The angel's big blue eyes widened, and she looked over my shoulder. "We don't use that word around here. You must be Tempest Crypt. We've been expecting you."

"I got delayed. Who's in charge around here?"

"We're run as a cooperative, like all Angel Force branches. Technically, we're all in charge." She beamed widely at me.

Of course. It was the same way they ran things back home. Although Dazielle was usually the one shouting the orders, and everyone deferred to her. "Okay, but who likes to pretend to be in charge?"

"That would be Sophie. She's so good at getting everyone organized and doing what they need to do. She's wonderful. She's been here over a hundred years."

"Great. Then let's go see Sophie."

"Of course. Let me complete your authorization form before we go through." The angel started filling in a sheet of paper with a feather quill.

"What am I being authorized to do?"

"Oh! We have a form for everything. This gives you a pass into the office and interview rooms. We don't want anyone to worry that you're in the wrong place."

I waited as the angel completed the form. She stamped it and handed me a badge. "Welcome to the team."

"I'm thrilled to be here." I attached the badge to my jacket.

"Right this way." She opened the hatch, and I followed her through.

There was a faint smell of vanilla and zesty orange as we walked past several rows of neat white desks. Angels sat at them, filling in stacks of paperwork. Every desk we passed, the angel looked up and gave us a smile. They were a lot more welcoming than the angels I knew back home.

I was led to a door, and the angel who escorted me knocked on it.

"Come in."

She opened the door and gestured me to go in. "I'll bring tea and cookies. I won't be a minute."

I peered in through the door. As I was expecting, the room was white, from the filing cabinets to the walls.

An enormous angel with a mass of blonde curls stood from her desk. She wore head to toe white, including an impressive pair of white stiletto boots. She strode over and grabbed my hand before gently ushering me into the room.

"You must be Tempest. It's so good to meet you." She pumped my hand. "I'm Sophie. When I heard from Dazielle that we had an expert demon catcher in Puzzlewood, it seemed the fated angels were shining on us. You're exactly what we need in this difficult situation."

"It sounds like you've got things under control. You've already arrested the killer." I sat in the seat she gestured to, and Sophie sat next to me.

"If you don't mind, we don't like that word."

"Killer?"

She winced, her smooth forehead crinkling. "It's so abrupt. We don't use the word murder, either. It upsets people."

"What do you call someone who's killed a person?"

"Unfortunate."

I choked out a laugh. "Whatever you say. So, you have the... unfortunate demon in custody?"

"Well, I hope we have. In all honesty, we got lucky catching him. One of my angels bumped into him when he was running from the scene of the crime.

She could tell something was wrong and restrained him until backup arrived."

"What kind of demon are we talking about?"

"He's a mammon underling. Third class. Not all that powerful."

Followers of the mammon school of demon misbehavior enjoyed taking expensive things and hoarding them. They loved anything sparkly. Basically, they were your every day, common thief with a side order of claws and scales. "What's a demon interested in stealing and tempting others doing killing someone?"

"My current theory is that the unfortunate individual was offered something in return for this gruesome act."

"Has he told you that?"

"Not yet."

"How big are we talking?"

"He's small. No taller than four feet. It's a mystery how he got in at all. We don't allow demons in Puzzlewood. Anyone tainted by a demon triggers the alerts on the magic barrier. When that happens, an angel locates the individual and gently persuades them to leave."

I rested a hand against my chest. Nothing had triggered when I'd entered Puzzlewood. It seemed the angels had a few weaknesses in their defenses.

Sophie looked up as the other angel appeared with an enormous tray. A large plate of cherry studded brownies sat on it along with two mugs of tea. She set everything on the desk, before smiling and heading out, leaving us alone again.

"Brownie?" Sophie passed me the plate.

I was starving. I'd been so busy hunting down Dad that I'd neglected to have lunch. "Thanks. So, tell me about this case. Someone was killed by this demon?"

"Not just someone, the renowned demonologist, Herbert Winkler. Have you heard of him?"

I ate a piece of my brownie and almost groaned at how delicious it was. It was the perfect combination of dark chocolate and cherry mixed in a mouth-watering combination. "Sure. He's published a load of books about dealing with demons. My sister stocks some in her store back home. You're saying this demon killed Herbert?"

"That's right. Herbert was taking a break from his tour. He was promoting his new book. Although that's not the most exciting thing the tour's promoting."

"What else was he promoting?"

"You haven't heard?" Sophie's blue eyes sparkled. "It's the most exciting thing to happen for a thousand years."

"Fill me in." I finished my brownie as Sophie bounced in her seat.

"Hold on to your hats. Herbert Winkler has created a cure for demonism."

I almost dropped the second brownie I'd picked up. "That's not possible. You can't cure someone who was born a certain way."

"According to Herbert, you can. It was the big selling point for his latest tour. In his new book, he details the experiments and treatments he provides to demons who no longer wish to be, well, demons."

I tilted my head. "What does a demon become when it's no longer a demon? An un-demon? A non-demon? Do they keep their powers?"

"Sadly, I haven't seen an advanced copy of the book, so I can't answer those questions."

"I can imagine there are a few hundred thousand demons in this world who aren't all that happy about this news."

"I expect some had concerns." Sophie sipped her tea. "Molvos, the demon who ended Herbert's life, must have targeted him because of that."

"No kidding. It's the perfect motive for this murder. I'm surprised a hoard of demons didn't take out Herbert the second he started trying to cure them of something they don't want to let go of."

"You'd be surprised. I dealt with a few demons back in the day, before I moved to Puzzlewood. They don't all like the fact they're demons. They want to be something else."

"Not the ones I've met. Most demons are happy causing chaos. All they want is to cause destruction, mayhem, and eat pizza."

Sophie smiled. "Sadly, that's also true. Especially about the pizza part. I've not yet met a demon who isn't incredibly greedy. Another brownie?"

"Yes, thanks." I took my third brownie. "So, how did this demon get to Herbert? You said he was taking a break from his tour. Was he here on his own?"

"No. He traveled with a small entourage. His business partner was with him, as were several of his friends, and an assistant. They're here at the station, waiting for an update. And they're keen for this matter to be swiftly resolved."

"How was Herbert killed? Dazielle said Molvos left a mess behind."

"He did." Sophie's face paled. "The party rented out a small house for their exclusive use while they were here. Molvos snuck in, and, well, I don't like to go into details, but he used his claws to great effect." She gulped down some tea.

"When did it happen?"

"Yesterday evening. Molvos was arrested at eight o'clock, which was a stroke of luck. We're usually all at home by then. The unfortunate event couldn't have happened much before that."

"What do you need me for? You've got the victim, you've got the demon, so it'll be simple to get physical proof of his involvement. Why don't you charge him and be done with it?"

"We're still processing the evidence. And Molvos is protesting his innocence," Sophie said.

"Sure he is. Most demons don't put their hands up to their crimes. You have to knock it out of them."

"Oh, no! We never support violence."

I shrugged. "Demons respond well to it. It's the language they all understand."

She shifted in her seat. "We don't want to get this wrong. None of my angels are experienced with serious crimes like this. We need everything done by the book. It's important the forms are completed and the right questions asked. We don't want Molvos to get off on a technicality."

I glanced at the large stack of paperwork on Sophie's desk. These angels sure loved their forms. "Have you checked his alibi?"

"We were hoping you could ask him questions and confirm that," she said.

"What have you done with him so far? You've had Molvos almost twenty-four hours."

Sophie jerked upright. "Which reminds me. I must complete a B1-48 form to extend Molvos' stay for another seventy-two hours."

"He's a murderer. You can hold him as long as you like."

She was already up and scribbling on a form. "Better to be safe. Like I said, this process must be appropriately recorded. Every form completed and stamped."

I tapped my fingers against the side of my mug. "You haven't asked Molvos anything about this crime?"

"No, we only asked him what he wanted for breakfast and lunch. He may be an unfortunate individual, but we don't want him to suffer."

"Of course. It's important to make it easy on the criminals."

Sophie nodded. "Dazielle said you know how to handle demons. I'd appreciate your input. Have you got time to question him now? We're open for another half an hour."

"Sure. There's no harm in having a chat."

"We'd be so grateful," Sophie said as she finished filling in the form and stamped it. "We're excited about having someone who's an expert in demons helping us. Dazielle told me you've assisted her in solving a number of cases. You must be her go-to person when it comes to bringing in demons who have crimes to answer for."

"I help her now and again," I said. And I'd probably help more if she was as obliging and friendly as Sophie and plied me with so many delicious brownies.

"Then it's settled. We finish our tea and brownies, then you can speak to Molvos and get his confession."

"That sounds good." I wiped my fingers clean on a napkin. "While I'm here, can you take a look at this picture? It's my—"

A loud, high-pitched wailing almost shattered my eardrums.

The office door was shoved open. A tiny, white-haired woman staggered in, her cheeks wet with tears. "Tell me it's not true. Tell me my boy isn't dead."

Sophie bit her lip, glancing at me, before she jumped to her feet. "Mrs. Winkler?"

The woman nodded. "I just heard the news. I was away on a walking vacation. I transported here the second I found out what happened." She grabbed Sophie's hands, her tiny fingers clutching on tight. "This must be a mistake. My Herbert can't be dead."

"I'm so sorry, Mrs. Winkler." Sophie patted her thin shoulder. "I'm afraid he is."

Mrs. Winkler began sobbing again, and Sophie wrapped her wings around her, the scent of vanilla becoming almost overpowering as she comforted the distraught woman.

I tucked my dad's picture back in my pocket. Now clearly wasn't the right time to ask about him.

"I'll take you to our visitor suite," Sophie said.

"I just want my boy back." Mrs. Winkler sniffed and dabbed at her cheeks. "Who would do such a terrible thing to him?"

"Don't worry. We've got the very best working this case." Sophie nodded at me. "We'll have the criminal charged and behind bars before you know it."

Mrs. Winkler glanced at me. "Please do everything you can to make sure my son's killer is brought to justice."

I shifted in my seat before nodding.

"Right this way," Sophie said. "Some of Herbert's friends are here. They'll be of comfort to you."

I stood and trailed along behind them as Sophie led Mrs. Winkler along a white corridor. She opened the door to another plush room, with comfy couches and soft music playing in the background.

"Oh! Virginia. You're here. And Jeremiah. Everyone's here." Mrs. Winkler staggered toward an attractive brunette with purple eyes, who engulfed her in a hug.

"Pearl! I'm so sorry this happened." Virginia's eyes clouded with tears as she clung to Mrs. Winkler.

I stood in the doorway next to Sophie as the group all talked at once and comforted the distraught woman.

"This is the touring party Herbert was traveling with," Sophie said softly. "The woman with the purple eyes is Virginia Lupin. She was dating Herbert but now acts as his personal assistant. The man next to her with blond hair was his best friend, Jeremiah Tombe."

"What about the ginger-haired guy?" I nodded to a thin, anxious looking guy with a shock of ginger hair and red eyes.

"That's Brendan Hazelton. He was Herbert's apprentice and training to become a demonologist. The man standing next to him is Saul Connelly. He managed Herbert's touring schedule."

"Did any of them see what happened to Herbert?"

"I've gathered brief information from each of them, so I know who they are, but again, I was hoping you would take the lead on questioning those close to the victim."

Mrs. Winkler wailed again, and my head began to throb. "Why don't I go chat with Molvos, see what I can get out of him?"

"That's an excellent idea. I just need to fill in the authorization form to let you speak to him, and then—"

There was a cry of alarm behind us.

"Whatever's going on now?" Sophie raced into the main office.

I was hot on her heels, pulling up short when I saw the chaos in the room. Angels were scattered in all directions, several cowering under their desks.

Bandit stood in the center of the room, her large wings extended around her and glitter spurting in all directions. She held a struggling angel around the throat.

"What are you doing?" I stalked toward her. "Put the angel down."

"Do you know this creature?" Sophie asked, her own wings extended.

"Unfortunately, I do," I said.

"Is she a criminal?" Sophie whispered.

"No! Although I wouldn't put anything past her. Bandit, why are you choking that angel?"

"She told me I had to fill in a form before I was allowed through," Bandit said. "I don't have time for that."

"The angels are nice." I gestured for her to let go of the angel she was choking. "Don't aggravate the friendly angels. They have brownies."

Bandit tutted as she dropped the angel to the floor. "As tempting as that is, the brownies will have to wait. I had to find you right away."

I helped the gasping angel to her feet. "What's the problem?"

Bandit smiled, flashing her sharp teeth. "It's gold star time for me. I've just found your dad."

Chapter 4

I blinked at Bandit, my brain freezing as I processed her words. "You've really found him?"

Sophie touched my arm, jogging me from my shock. "We're not keen on unregulated fairies in Puzzlewood." She turned to Bandit. "Do you have your authorization card?"

"What's that?" Bandit shot an irritated glance at Sophie.

"You need it, so we can determine your level of powers and make appropriate arrangements. I can process the form tomorrow and have you assessed."

"I don't need an authorization card. I'm with Tempest. She'll vouch for me." Bandit kept her attention on me. "Come on. We need to move before we lose him."

I looked at Sophie. "I have to go."

"Wait! What about the interview with Molvos?"

"I'll be back later."

"We close in half an hour."

I shook my head. I was already heading toward the door, Bandit leading the way. "Then I'll be back tomorrow."

I ignored Sophie's protests as I raced out the main door. "Where did you find him?" I asked Bandit.

"In a bar," she said.

"You've been looking for him all this time? I figured you'd gone off to the water park."

"As tempted as I was to abandon you when you were so rude to me, I don't abort a mission."

I felt a little guilty for thinking so badly of Bandit. Maybe she wasn't such a terrible fairy after all. "How does he look?"

"Not great. Rough around the edges. And he could do with a bath. At first, I didn't recognize him. He doesn't look much like that picture you've been showing around. That must be why people didn't identify him."

My gut clenched. Maybe the ten years he'd been away had been hard. Just what had he been doing all this time?

I caught hold of Bandit's arm as we reached the entrance of the Tipsy Tipple Bar. "What should I do when I see him?"

She pursed her lips. "What do you want to do?"

"Hug him. Hit him and ask why he abandoned us all those years ago. Find out what he's been doing for the last ten years. Take him home and forgive him." I ran a hand down my face. "I don't know. What if he doesn't want to see me?"

"You think he abandoned your awesome family because he wasn't happy?" Bandit shook her head. "You Crypt witches are amazing. I had fun while I was with Aurora, and you aren't so terrible to be around when you ditch the smelly hellhound. Your dad will want to be back in your life."

I rocked back on my heels, my hand on my stomach. I'd waited so long to see my dad. Now the moment was here, I wanted to chicken out.

"Hey, quit being a loser. Get in the bar and see your dad." Bandit shoved me toward the door.

"What are you going to do?"

"Lurk in the shadows. Don't worry. I'll be around if you need me. He's sitting at the bar on the left. Now go." She shoved me so hard that I slammed into the door and staggered through it.

It took a few seconds for my eyes to adjust to the gloomy interior. The ceiling was low, with dark beams running across it and a large open fireplace at one end of the room. Small round tables were set out, and the bar was at the back.

The place wasn't busy, with only a dozen people sitting around sipping on their drinks.

I tugged on the hem of my jacket before walking to the bar. I kept my gaze forward, wanting a few seconds before I turned to my dad and introduced myself back into his life.

A tall barman walked over and nodded at me. "What will it be?"

"Do you do lemon drops?"

"Of course. House double?"

"Sure, that'll be great." I placed money on the bar and tried to calm my racing heartbeat. It only seemed to get faster.

I turned my head an inch and studied the man who sat four bar stools away, hunched over an almost empty glass of whiskey. He had sandy brown hair that curled at the nape of his neck. He wore black jeans, boots, and a scuffed leather jacket. I needed to get a good look at his face to be sure it was him.

The barman placed my drink down and took the money. "You passing through?"

"I'm staying for a few days," I said.

"This isn't a usual tourist hang out," the barman said. "You might prefer the bars in the main shopping mall. You get a friendlier clientele."

"This is fine for me," I said.

"Suit yourself." He walked away and refilled my dad's glass without him asking.

"Thanks," my dad mumbled.

"I still think you should get out of here for a while." The barman picked up on a conversation they must have been having before I arrived.

He shrugged. "I keep telling you it's got nothing to do with me."

"You know the angels will want to talk to you."

"Of course. They always look my way when there's trouble in this perky nightmare of a place."

My fingers tightened around my glass. What kind of trouble was he talking about?

"You'd better not be involved in this murder," the barman said.

My head jerked up, and I stared straight at my dad. They must be discussing Herbert. I turned away and shielded my face with my hair. Why would my dad be involved in that?

"The angels around here may be as useless as a one-legged dwarf in a butt kicking contest, but they'll come find you eventually," the barman said. "And if you're in here when they do, I don't want trouble."

"When do I ever cause you trouble?"

"Last month, when you sank most of a bottle of whiskey and tried to start a fight with that nice young couple."

"You're mistaking me for someone else. I'd never do that. This is my favorite place to drink."

"It's your only place to drink. You've been barred from everywhere else."

My dad simply grunted.

This had me confused. He was never a big drinker. Sure, he liked a glass of wine now and again and would often stop by for a lemon drop in my club, but it sounded like he spent most of his time in here. And why had he been barred from every other place in Puzzlewood? This wasn't the man I knew.

"You should make it easy on the angels. Go talk to them now. You can tell them where you were when that guy was killed, and they'll leave you alone," the barman said.

"Why should I help them? They've done nothing but hassle me since I've been here. Besides, they've already got someone for the murder. They won't come looking for me."

"Yeah, and we both know who they've got. He'll lead the angels straight to you."

"Molvos won't say a word. He knows better than that."

The barman shook his head. "It's your funeral, my friend." He strolled away to the other end of the bar.

I swallowed, my throat tight. I should say something, but the man sitting near me felt like a stranger. This wasn't my dad.

"Did you get most of that?" My dad's voice was a low rumble in his chest.

I tensed and glanced around. "Are you talking to me?"

"You were the only one listening to our conversation. Hear something of interest?"

This was it. It was time to show him who I was. I lifted my head, my heart pounding so hard my ears rang. I met his gaze and stared straight at him.

His eyes flicked over me. "Like the barman said, you shouldn't be in here."

I jerked back in my seat. "You... you don't know me?"

"Are you supposed to be someone special?"

I continued to stare at him. He was kidding. He really didn't recognize me?

"What's wrong with you? Why are you staring at me like that?" He rolled his shoulders and glanced over his shoulder. "You look like you've seen a ghost."

"No, I can see that you're very much alive." I turned fully toward him. Maybe he was drunk, or the bad lighting meant he couldn't see me properly. "We haven't seen each other for a long time."

A flicker of what looked like recognition crossed his face. "I meet a lot of people. I travel around. I guess you're not memorable to me." He returned to his whiskey and took a sip.

How was this possible? I didn't look that different. And now I'd gotten a good look at him, this was definitely my dad. Sure, he was rough around the edges. He had lines around his eyes and a good week's worth of stubble on his chin, but it was him.

"You're still staring," he muttered. "Go hassle someone else."

I couldn't take this any longer. Blow the consequences with Frank and the deal they'd made all those years ago, I had to get him to see who I was.

I climbed off the stool and took a step toward him.

The barman returned and tapped the back of my hand, making me pause. "Hold it right there, missy. I don't want any trouble."

"You won't get any trouble from me," I said.

"I was talking to Abel," the barman said.

"I have nothing to do with this. She's the one prodding me," he said.

I tilted my head. "Did you say Abel?"

"That's my name, sweetheart. Don't wear it out." My dad downed his whiskey, tossed money on the counter, and walked out without a backward glance.

I stared after him. Why was he using a different name?

"Hey, a word of advice. Stay away from Abel Cross," the barman said.

I turned to face him. "Is that his real name?"

The barman's broad forehead wrinkled. "Sure it is. Are you okay? You look like you're about to pass out."

I staggered back to the stool and sat on it. "I've had a shock."

"Yeah, Abel often has that effect on people. That guy is bad to the bone."

I shook my head. I couldn't process what had just happened. "I thought I knew him. From a long time ago."

"Maybe your paths have crossed," the barman said. "Abel gets around. He works as a freelance bounty hunter. He gets paid to do all the dirty work. And so long as he gets the money he's owed, he doesn't care what he has to do for it."

I pressed my fingers against my forehead. My dad chased down bad guys? That line of work wasn't so different from what I did. Though I didn't do the dirty work and rarely broke the law. If ever I did, it was always for a good cause. My stomach churned.

"Have another drink," the barman said. "And if that enormous fairy skulking in the shadows has anything to do with you, you need to tell her to come out. She's scaring off my remaining customers."

"Sure. And yes to the drink." I gestured Bandit over.

"That looked like an interesting chat with Artie." She leaned against the bar and flashed her sharp teeth at the barman. "This is a private conversation."

He scowled at her before stomping away.

I sipped my drink, my hand shaking as I lowered the glass.

Bandit nudged me with her elbow. "Your dad wasn't happy that you found him?"

"He didn't recognize me," I said. "I stared him right in the eye, and he didn't even blink. He acted like I was a stranger."

"Maybe you've changed more than you realize," Bandit said. "Were you really fat as a kid? Did you have fuzzy hair and braces?"

"No!"

"Did you tell him your name?"

"I didn't get the chance," I said. "And I got side-tracked when the barman called him Abel. That's not his name. Unless my dad has a twin he never mentioned, this just got strange."

"Stranger than when he walked out of your life ten years ago?"

I grimaced. "Thanks for the reminder."

"Hey, is your name Tempest?" the barman yelled from the end of the bar.

"That's me," I said.

"I've got an incoming message for you on my snow globe." He strode over, the scowl still on his face. "Those wretched angels. They think it's okay to hassle my customers. Keep it short. I'm waiting for a call." He thumped the snow globe in front of me and walked off.

I touched the globe with my finger to activate the message.

"This is an automated message for Tempest Crypt." A sweet, high-pitched voice trilled. "We have new information on the suspect being held in custody. He has informed us he has an associate who is implicated in the unfortunate incident involving Herbert Winkler. His name is Abel Cross."

"Holy fairy lights on a stick." Bandit shoved me so hard that I fell off the stool.

I clutched the edge of the bar and grabbed the snow globe.

The message continued. "Please find Mr. Cross and bring him to the Angel Force office at your earliest convenience. We open tomorrow at nine. Angels' greetings to you."

"Abel Cross?" Bandit tapped her finger on the top of the bar. "That's the name your dad now uses."

I nodded, my face hot as a shudder ran through me. My dad was involved with this murder.

This case just got personal.

Chapter 5

I kept re-playing the message the angels had sent me. My dad couldn't be involved with killing Herbert. Sure, it sounded like he'd turned into some kind of seedy, double-dealing bounty hunter, but a murderer? I couldn't get my head around that. I didn't want to.

"Where are we going?" Bandit strutted next to me as I headed out of the bar.

"Back to interview Molvos," I said. "Make him tell the truth. My dad's not involved in this. We have to get Molvos to confess to the murder, so Dad's in the clear."

"You think the angels have gotten this wrong?"

"Of course, they have. My dad's no killer. Molvos is lying to save his own scaly skin."

"Maybe ten years ago he wasn't a ruthless, bloodthirsty tyrant. But now..."

"People change, but they don't change that much."

"Maybe someone forced your dad to do it. He could have acted under duress."

I scowled as I considered this. Dad's slide into darkness could have something to do with Frank.

What if he'd been forced to work for Frank in exchange for keeping me and the rest of the family safe? Dad would do anything to protect the family, maybe even murder.

"Let's speak to Molvos," I said.

"And if he doesn't instantly confess?"

Gah! Why did this fairy have to keep prodding at me? "Then I'll think of something else. My dad is innocent."

We stopped outside the main door of the Angel Force building. The lights were off, and there was a closed sign up.

"You are kidding me? They don't have anyone on duty? What if there are problems with the prisoners?" I tapped on the glass, hoping to see an angel appear.

"I could break us in." Bandit grabbed the door knob.

Two jets of brilliant white light shot out of the small white stone angels that sat on either side of the door. The light blasted Bandit off her feet in a shower of sparks and glitter.

"Wowzers! What was that?" Bandit sprawled on the ground as the light pinned her down and ran over her.

"Thank you for your interest in the Puzzlewood branch of Angel Force," a friendly disembodied female voice said. "We are currently closed. Our operating hours are nine o'clock in the morning to five in the evening. Please return during those hours, and we will be happy to help you. Angels' greetings to you."

The white light faded, and Bandit shot to her feet. "That's not fair. Angels aren't supposed to attack people."

I eyed the door with caution. "We still need to get in and see Molvos." I paced around the outside of the building trying to find a way in, but it was no use. Every door and window we tried gave out the same automated response, telling us to go away in the kindest possible way.

"Tempest, is that you?" Sophie walked around the side of the building dressed in a white lounge suit, her blonde curls piled on top of her head. "What are you doing here so late?"

"Is there any chance you can let us inside to speak to Molvos?" I asked.

She shook her head. "No, that's not possible. But I'm glad to find it's just you and your fairy here. I get an alert when the angel rays trigger. I thought we may have an intruder trying to break in."

"You should have a warning sign up about those ray things," Bandit said. "I singed a wing."

"Oh! A thousand apologies," Sophie said. "Most people know about the security angels. Of course, I should have considered the health and safety aspect. The rays aren't fatal, though."

"They felt fatal when I was pinned down by them," Bandit muttered.

"I'll get a sign up as soon as possible," Sophie said. "We must put safety before anything else."

"So, about Molvos," I asked, "it would be a big help if I could see him right away."

"I am sorry, but it's against regulation 518C part three. No one can interview suspects outside of regulation hours."

"Can't you bend that important sounding regulation just this once? I need to deal with this... unfortunate situation with Herbert."

"We all want that. But Molvos is already tucked up in bed. He had a big dinner and said he was tired. He'll be no good to you now."

"It sounds more like you're running a hotel than an interrogation unit," Bandit said.

"We don't interrogate people." Sophie blinked her large eyes slowly. "You get more flies with honey. Treat the criminals with respect and courtesy, and they respond in kind."

"Does that mean he's confessed to what he did?" I asked.

"Not yet." Sophie pursed her lips. "You got the information about his possible accomplice?"

"Abel Cross," I said. "I met him today."

"Then you'll understand why I'm not surprised he could be involved with this situation," Sophie said.

"I'm yet to form an opinion of him. Why do you think Abel's involved?" I asked.

Sophie smiled broadly. "I can tell you all about it. Why don't you come stay with me tonight? We can discuss the case and make plans for tomorrow when we re-open the office."

"No, I appreciate the offer, but we've got a room in a local motel." I wasn't sure I could stand being around Sophie's sunny disposition for long. She was like Aurora on happy steroids.

"You must. I'd consider it an honor if you'd dine with me as well," Sophie said. "I have a charming apartment a few streets away and plenty of room. Both of you are welcome. I'm making macaroni and cheese and a homemade caramel apple crumble with ice cream for dessert."

"We should definitely go with the angel," Bandit said.

"Please do. I'll be tempted to eat it all if I don't have company. Angels really shouldn't be gluttons. It goes against our code of conduct."

"I could go for some delicious dessert," Bandit said. "Let's stay with the angel. It could be fun."

My mouth twisted to the side. I wasn't so sure about spending time with Sophie. She seemed nice enough but came with that sickeningly sweet aftertaste I always got when I hung around angels.

"You'd be doing me a great favor," Sophie said. "I'll get to tell everybody that I had the great demon catcher, Tempest Crypt, in my apartment."

"Great demon catcher?" Bandit snorted a laugh. "Is that what she told you she is?"

"Hey! I can hold my own when it comes to demons," I said.

"I don't doubt that for a second," Sophie said. "And I'd love to hear all your stories. Although I'm not keen on the gory details. Please, come for dinner."

"We don't want to hurt the nice angel's feelings," Bandit muttered in far too loud a stage whisper. "Let's go have some free food."

I guess it couldn't hurt to eat. And we'd get to discuss the case. I'd also be able to learn more about my dad and what the angels knew about his past. "Thanks. Dinner sounds good."

Sophie clapped her hands together. "I'm delighted. Right this way. I was making the finishing touches to dinner when I got the alert that the station was being tampered with."

We walked along as Sophie pointed out various stores we had to visit once we'd sorted out the *unfortunate incident,* as she kept calling Herbert's murder.

We arrived outside a large apartment complex and headed up to the penthouse.

Sophie stepped out of the elevator and took off her white sneakers. "Shoes by the door if you don't mind."

I yanked off my boots and placed them in the corner. I could see why she didn't want anyone stomping dirt everywhere. The whole place was white. Why wasn't I surprised?

"Oooh! You have birds." Bandit dashed to a large golden cage. Sitting inside were two plump white turtle doves.

"That's Eros and Iris. I named them after Greek goddesses. They're my messenger birds. They can travel great distances without tiring. I use them when the snow globes aren't active or if I ever need to send a secure message. I've had them for years. They're my best friends."

Bandit tapped on the side of the cage. "They look tasty."

Sophie's eyes widened.

"She's joking," I said. Most likely, Bandit wasn't joking if the look on her face was anything to go by, but we didn't need to alarm Sophie.

"Take a seat. I'll bring out nibbles. Dinner won't be long." Sophie shot a worried look at Bandit before hurrying away.

"Leave the birds alone," I whispered.

"Look at them. I bet they're delicious with some marinade. Sophie won't mind if I take one. She seems very hospitable." Her hand crept toward the cage door.

"Step away from the cage," I said. "We need to keep this angel on our side. She could have useful information about my dad. Besides, I thought you only ate things the color of nature."

"What's more natural than this? Sophie clearly overfeeds them. I doubt they can even fly they're so fat. Ouch!" Bandit yanked her finger out of the cage as one of the turtle doves scuttled over and nipped her.

"That'll teach you to meddle with the tubby birds." I turned away and walked around the apartment. There were two large white couches set around a fireplace. There was also a bookshelf and a writing desk in one corner. A large shaggy white rug sat on the floor.

I spun around at the sound of a squawk.

Bandit stood in front of the cage, her hands clasped behind her back.

"What did you do?" I stalked over.

She shrugged and shook her head.

I stared at her mouth, which looked worryingly full. "Let the bird go."

She raised her eyebrows, and her eyes widened.

"I'll tell Aurora that you hurt the cute bird." I stepped forward and held my hands out.

Bandit rolled her eyes before opening her mouth.

I grabbed the damp looking turtle dove and rubbed her dry on my top. Other than looking a bit soggy, she wasn't harmed.

The bird nipped my palm and dug her claws into my wrist.

"Quit it. I'm trying to keep you alive," I said.

"Aurora would understand if I ate one," Bandit said. "If she was here, she'd let me eat the dumb bird. It's just like you eating a chicken."

"You know that's not true. Aurora's a big animal lover. She'd be horrified if she learned about this."

"Which isn't going to happen, is it?" Bandit jabbed me in the ribs with a wing tip. "I didn't do anything wrong."

"Only because I caught you before you swallowed." I placed the unhappy bird back in the cage and closed the door.

"Here we are." Sophie returned with a tray full of delicious looking nibbles. "Have a few of these. I need to lay the table and get everything plated up. I'll also make up the guest rooms, so they're ready when you want to retire. Make yourselves at home while I'm busy."

"Thanks. These look great." I dragged Bandit over to the food and distracted her with the cheesy sticks and pastry bites provided by Sophie.

"Goodness, you've eaten them all," Sophie said when she returned a few moments later. "Would you like more?"

"Yes, please," Bandit said.

"Let's wait for dinner," I said.

"Then you're in luck," Sophie said. "Right this way. Dinner is served."

"Shall I let your birds out?" Bandit said, a look of innocence on her sparkly face. "They look like they could do with a fly."

"Of course," Sophie said. "I usually let them out in the evenings. I wasn't sure if you'd want them flying around while we were eating."

"Maybe they should stay in the cage for tonight," I said.

"Don't be mean, Tempest. Those birds need exercise." Bandit hurried back to the cage and opened the door. She walked back to me and nudged me with her elbow. "You never know, one might accidentally fly into my mouth."

"Don't you dare," I muttered as I took my seat at the table.

The table presentation wouldn't have been amiss in the Michelin starred restaurant. There was silver cutlery, crystal glasses, and a pristine white tablecloth.

"It's nice to have company to share my meal with." Sophie sat in her own seat. "Would either of you like to give thanks before we begin?"

I glanced at Bandit. "Um. Well, I guess—"

"Yes! I will," Bandit said. "Let's join hands."

This could be interesting. We joined hands, and I lowered my head.

Bandit cleared her throat. "I'd like to begin by thanking Sophie for being gracious enough to let us into her home tonight. The food smells delicious, as do the birds."

I squeezed her hand.

"I'd also like to give thanks to Aurora, who took me in when no one else would. It was a hard life being a fur shedding ginger cat, but I made the best friend a fairy could ever find. I'd also like to give thanks to Tempest for not being too terrible to be around."

I dug my fingernails into her hand.

"And finally, I'd like to give thanks to my awesome glittery wings, amazing flying skills, and humbleness. Let's eat, shall we?"

Sophie's face showed her surprise as we dropped hands. "Thank you, Bandit. That was most illuminating." She served the tantalizing smelling macaroni and cheese, and we all tucked in.

"I'm interested to learn more about Abel Cross," I said. "Why do you think he's involved with what happened to Herbert?"

"Molvos slipped up when I was talking to him," she said. "He mentioned his name. Of course, the second Abel Cross is involved, you know trouble won't be far behind."

"How long has he lived in Puzzlewood?" I asked.

"He comes and goes. He sometimes rents a room from one of the bars in Puzzlewood, but his... freelance work takes him out of the area. I have to admit to breathing a relieved sigh whenever I hear he has a job."

"He's a bounty hunter?"

Sophie nodded. "That's right. But not the kind you'd want anything to do with. Most bounty hunters work to ensure the streets are safe for everyone. That's a noble code all good bounty hunters live by."

"And it has nothing to do with the huge sums of money they get paid for bringing in the trouble makers," Bandit said.

"I'm sure some hunters are motivated by the financial side of their work," Sophie said. "Abel certainly is. He takes the jobs that pay well but often put him on the wrong side of the law. Our paths have crossed many times."

"You've arrested him?" I asked.

"He's never been charged with anything," Sophie said. "But that's only because of lack of evidence. He doesn't just deal with criminals; he gets paid to frighten people. He's a hired thug for whoever will pay the right price."

The more I learned about Abel Cross, the more my worry grew. Something terrible must have happened to my dad to turn him to the dark side.

"Molvos is pointing the finger at him for killing Herbert?" Bandit asked.

"He didn't directly accuse him of that unfortunate incident," Sophie said. "But I was surprised to find Molvos involved in this crime. As you rightly pointed out, Tempest, he's more interested in obtaining material items. I expected to find him in the possession of things he'd stolen. This is most out of character for Molvos. You know demons better than I do. Would he have strayed so far off the path?"

"All demons have a twisted side," I said. "Maybe Herbert put up a fight when Molvos was trying to take his things. He retaliated and Molvos killed him. It would help if I could see the body."

Sophie swallowed and lowered her fork. "Of course. I didn't think. It'll take me some time to get the right authorization."

"How long?"

"A week."

I stabbed at my macaroni and cheese. I didn't want to wait around a week to see a corpse. I didn't even want to see the body, but maybe the angels missed something. They seemed inexperienced when it came to dealing with serious crime.

"If it's any consolation, we have examined Herbert for clues. My angels are very thorough."

"Have you also examined Molvos' claws for blood?" I asked.

Sophie bit her bottom lip. "Yes. But he must have cleaned up before he left the crime scene."

"You've got no direct evidence that Molvos killed Herbert?"

She lined up the salt and pepper shakers before gently shrugging. "Not yet. But I'm confident of a confession. And if this crime also puts Abel in prison, then so much the better. He has long been a thorn in the side of Puzzlewood. It'll be no loss to have him off the streets."

Something warm and wet landed on my head. I glanced up to see a turtle dove sitting on the chandelier above the table, its feathery white behind aimed at me.

"Oh, my goodness! I must apologize for my bird." Sophie jumped to her feet and passed me her napkin. "They're usually so well-behaved when I have guests. I've trained them to go to the toilet inside their cages. Eros, what were you thinking?"

The other bird swooped over my head and landed a well-aimed poop on my shoulder.

"Eros! Iris! This is so embarrassing. Stop misbehaving." Sophie flapped her hands at the birds. "These are our guests. We don't poop on guests."

"Are you sure you don't want me to eat them now?" Bandit whispered.

I grimaced as the poop slid down my arm.

"Tempest, I'm so sorry. Let me get you a change of clothes," Sophie said.

"It's fine. This will wash out. I'll just use your bathroom." I stood from my seat, careful not to move my head in case the first poop slid down my face.

"Of course. Straight down the hall, second door on the left." Sophie was busy ferrying the misbehaving turtle doves back to their cage.

I hurried to the bathroom and closed the door behind me. I needed a few minutes alone. The news about my dad being involved with Molvos was bad. Everything suggested he'd turned to crime since leaving Willow Tree Falls. I needed to know the motivation behind it. What caused him to become so dark?

I sponged out my top as best I could and washed the bird poop out of my hair before returning to the table and finishing what was left of my meal. It looked like Bandit had been helping herself to my mac and cheese while I'd been gone.

After a delicious helping of caramel apple crumble, I was overtaken by an enormous yawn and found myself blinking heavy eyes.

"I suggest an early night for us all," Sophie said. "In the morning, everything will seem much brighter. You can speak to Molvos and clear this up. Puzzlewood will be safe again."

"That sounds like a plan," I said. However, I had my own plan. I couldn't wait until the morning, not now I knew my dad was involved with this. Once everyone was asleep, I was sneaking out, breaking into the Angel Force building, and getting to the bottom of this.

We said our goodnights, and Sophie whisked away the dishes, refusing my feeble offer of help.

I'd only been in my bedroom for five minutes before Bandit shoved the door open without knocking.

"I'm bored. What are you doing?"

I gestured her inside, and she shut the door behind her. "Has Sophie gone in her bedroom yet?"

"She has. A couple of minutes ago. Why?"

"Once she's asleep, I'm going back to speak to Molvos."

Bandit's eyes gleamed, and she rubbed her hands together. "Can I come with you?"

"No, you need to stay here and keep an eye on Sophie."

"There's no fun in that," Bandit said. "Besides, it's not safe to leave me here. I might eat those birds."

"I'm almost tempted to let you after the double pooping incident during dinner," I said. "But I need you to cause a distraction in case Sophie wakes and wonders where I am."

"What am I supposed to do, lie to an angel?" She shook her head.

"I bet it won't be the first time you've done such a thing."

"This is very true." Bandit crossed her arms over her chest. "What if Sophie sets her chubby feathered friends on me if she catches me?"

"More food for you if that does happen."

"Huh! I guess so. Okay, I can stay here." Bandit sat on my bed and groaned. "Have you tried these beds, though? They're awesome. So comfortable."

"I don't care about how comfortable the beds are."

Bandit grabbed my hand and yanked me down next to her. "You really should. I'm pretty sure the pillows are full of angel feathers. They have that weird vanilla scent Sophie exudes. I've had to resist the urge to lick her all night to see if she tastes as good as she smells."

"I have an allergy to angels and their feathers," I said.

"You're only angry at Sophie because she didn't say nice things about your dad."

"Which is why I need to find out for myself just how involved he is with this murder." I lay back on the bed and yawned. It really was a comfortable bed, and it smelt amazing.

"I'll get you a blanket." Bandit grabbed a soft cream throw and covered me with it.

"I don't want a blanket." I yawned again, my eyes feeling heavy. Maybe a power nap wouldn't be a bad thing.

I'd have half an hour, then I'd head out and interrogate Molvos.

Chapter 6

I twitched my nose as something pinged against it.

My eyes flicked open. Bandit loomed over me, about to flick my nose again with her finger.

I yelped and rolled out of her reach. "Why are you on my bed?"

"Fairies don't need much sleep. I got bored. And watching you snooze is entertaining. You talk in your sleep."

"I do not."

"You do. You said Rhett's name a lot."

My cheeks grew warm. I threw aside the throw that covered me and sat up. "What time is it?"

"Seven in the morning."

My mouth fell open. "I've been asleep all night? I only meant to have a thirty-minute nap. Why didn't you wake me?"

"You looked so cute when you were asleep," Bandit said. "That frown line between your eyebrows vanishes when you relax."

I rubbed my forehead. "I don't have frown lines."

"You do. It's so cute. I almost didn't want to wake you, but I got bored rigid with no one to talk to."

I hopped off the bed. I was still wearing my clothes from the day before. Even though I was annoyed at wasting so much time, I'd had an amazing night of sleep. That bed was the most comfortable I'd ever slept in. Still, I should be clearing my dad's name and solving Herbert's murder, not snoozing on some deliciously snug bed in an angel's house.

There was a knock on the bedroom door, and Sophie pushed it open. "Good morning, you two. Did you sleep well?" She looked immaculate, with perfect makeup and pristine curls framing her face.

"We had an excellent night," Bandit said. "Tempest was just saying what a great night she had."

Sophie smiled warmly. "I'm pleased to hear that. I always like to make sure my guests have an enjoyable stay when they visit."

"I got so sleepy right after dessert," I said. "I couldn't keep my eyes open."

"A carb loaded meal will do that to you," Bandit said.

"I rarely sleep that soundly, though. And I don't usually get tired until gone midnight. I'm usually working late at the club. It was so weird."

"That may have something to do with the mayberry juice in your drink." Sophie looked away, and a blush crossed her cheeks. "The berries have a gentle sedative effect."

My eyebrows shot up. "Are you saying you drugged me?"

"Oh, no! Nothing that extreme. But I always like to make sure my guests feel relaxed and comfortable in my home. The mayberries help you feel mellow and chilled out."

Bandit roared with laughter. "She totally drugged you. The berries had zero effect on me."

"I heard you wandering around in the night. I hope everything was to your satisfaction." Sophie glanced over her shoulder.

"Sure. Although I could do with some breakfast," Bandit said.

"Then right this way," Sophie said. "I hope you like waffles and pancakes."

"I'm more a fruit kind of person in the morning," Bandit said. "But I can handle a waffle."

"Of course. Whatever you want," Sophie said.

I shook my head, still amazed this angel had the audacity to drug me. Had she done it deliberately because she'd figured out I wasn't planning on sticking around last night? Maybe there was more to this angel than her saccharine sweet smile.

I found it hard to be angry with her. I felt like I'd just spent a week at a spa being pampered. Maybe it wasn't so terrible to grab a decent night of sleep. At least now, I could focus on getting to the bottom of this mystery.

My eyes widened as I walked into the kitchen and stared at the spread on the table. There were waffles, pancakes, platters of fruit, yogurt, cereal, toast, and crumpets.

"Am I missing anything?" Sophie asked. "I didn't know what you liked for breakfast, so I made a selection."

"This looks amazing." I settled into my seat and accepted a delicious smelling cup of freshly ground coffee from Sophie. "This isn't drugged, is it?"

"No, I promise. We all need to be full of pep to deal with the unfortunate incident today." She gestured for me to take a sip. "And I did feel bad about stopping you from speaking to Molvos last night."

"We could have made progress already if I'd gotten in to see him," I said.

"I understand that. So, I begged one of my angels to go in early today. She's currently completing the authorization paperwork so you can interview Molvos as soon as we get there. There'll be no delays."

"You sure have a lot of paperwork to complete before you do anything around here." Bandit stuffed a handful of strawberries into her mouth.

"It's important there's a paper trail for everything," Sophie said. "We don't want anyone accused of something they haven't done. When you have the paperwork to prove the appropriate steps were taken when dealing with a criminal, you can't go wrong. We don't want a repeat of the incident in 1865."

"What happened in 1865?" Bandit asked.

Sophie's cheeks flushed again. "It was before my time."

"Go on, who messed up?"

Sophie let out a soft sigh. "I was graduating from my class when it happened. Have you ever heard of Volker Bladen?"

Bandit choked on her food. "The famous pixie eater? Of course."

I raised a hand. "I haven't."

"This is an epic story," Bandit said. "It all started... no, Sophie, you tell it. I haven't heard an original account of what went down, only second-hand gossip. You met Volker?"

"No. I never met him." She pressed her lips together before nodding. "Puzzlewood was expanding its operations at that time. I was being mentored by another angel who'd worked the area for fifty years. A large workforce of pixies was drafted in to help with the expansion work. Suddenly, they started vanishing. At first, it was thought they simply flew off and found other work. Then the wings started showing up."

"Pinned on people's doors," Bandit said, a disturbingly gleeful smile on her face.

I wrinkled my nose. "That's gross. Someone was taking pixies and pulling their wings off?"

"Before they died." Sophie shook her head. "It was such a terrible crime."

"And this Volker guy was arrested for pixie abuse?" I asked.

"He was found with a heap of dead pixies in his apartment and some wings," Bandit said. "I never figured out why he wasn't sent away for life."

"Because the angels in Puzzlewood made mistakes," Sophie said. "A form was incorrectly completed, and some crucial evidence was mislabeled."

"Ouch! Double mess up," Bandit said.

"It didn't help that Volker had an amazing lawyer. He ripped the case apart, called the angels incompetent, and the jury let Volker go on a technicality."

I winced. I could understand now why she loved her forms so much. The angels' mess up left a vicious killer on the loose.

"The last I heard about Volker, he'd retired to some tropical island," Bandit said. "The guy is untouchable."

"Sadly so, unless he gets caught committing more crimes. Anyway, that's all in the past. No more slip ups in Puzzlewood, thanks to our excellent forms," Sophie said. "We'll have breakfast, then you can question Molvos about the unfortunate incident. Perhaps after he's had a night in a cell thinking about what he did, he'll be receptive to talking to you."

"Not if you feed him a breakfast this delicious," Bandit said.

"Oh, he doesn't get anything this nice," Sophie said. "We serve a basic cooked breakfast. Three rounds of bacon, sausages, and eggs. And toast on the side if they want it." She leaned closer. "And we only give suspects instant coffee."

"That sounds like torture," I said.

After stuffing myself so full I could barely move, I took a quick shower and dressed before heading out with Sophie and Bandit back to the Angel Force office.

As promised, three long forms had been completed. All I needed to do was sign them in triplicate before I got access to Molvos.

Sophie left me in an interview room, and I paced around as I waited for Molvos to arrive. I needed to keep my cool. I had to get this demon to reveal his involvement with this murder and why he thought it was okay to frame my dad for his crime.

The door opened a couple of minutes later. A short, squat, dark green demon with overly long arms and short sharp claws on the ends of his fingers and toes appeared, followed by Sophie.

He smiled when he saw me. "You're definitely not an angel."

"You are going to behave yourself, Molvos," Sophie said as she gestured to a chair. "This is Tempest Crypt. She's here to question you about what happened with Herbert Winkler. It's important you cooperate with her."

"I've been nothing but cooperative since I've been here." Molvos settled in his seat and smiled up at Sophie.

She nodded at me. "I'll leave you both to it. Any problems, just shout."

I waited until the door closed before focusing on Molvos. He didn't give off the aura of a dark twisted demon intent on death and chaos. He swung his short legs on the chair and looked at me, a curious expression on his face.

"Tell me why you killed Herbert Winkler," I said.

He jerked back in his seat. "I didn't. I keep telling the angels I'm innocent."

"You were just in the wrong place at the wrong time?"

"Exactly. I liked Professor Winkler. He was a brilliant man."

"Even though he claimed to have found a cure for demonism?"

"Yes! I liked him because of that. And he's got me to thank for the cure." Molvos puffed out his chest and tapped a finger against it.

"What do you mean?"

"I worked with Professor Winkler."

"You were helping him to find a cure?"

"That's right. Professor Winkler needed demons to volunteer as part of his trials. I was happy to get involved."

"Why?"

"I don't want to be a demon. All the scales and meanness, it's just not me. I want to be a good guy. Settle down, have a family, maybe start my own business."

That sounded most un-demon like. "Why don't you want to be a demon?"

He swung his legs some more. "I don't want people looking at me with fear in their eyes and running away. I want a quiet life. I want people to like me."

"What would you do if you weren't a demon?"

"I thought about opening a pizza parlor. I love pizza. I make great pizza."

This interview wasn't going how I imagined it would. "So, you had no problem with Herbert?"

"Thanks to him, I'm now a decent guy. I have no desire to hurt anyone or cause mischief. It's thanks to the clinical trials I went through. I have no bad feelings against Herbert. He changed my life for the better. And he had plans to do it for any demon who wanted a fresh start. A chance to try something different. Make the best of themselves."

"That can't include many demons. This cure put a target on Herbert's back. Most demons who heard about these tests would want to stop to them."

"I'm sure some would," Molvos said.

"Do any demons spring to mind?" I asked. "Have you heard anything on the grapevine that someone was coming for him?"

He scratched his nose with the tip of a claw. "There were problems during his recent tour. Professor Winkler mentioned it during the latest tests he ran to see how the cure was taking. There have been protests, and not just from demons. A number of magic using individuals don't think his cure is right."

"I'm sort of on their side. Being a demon is in your nature. You were born a demon. You can't help but be a demon. Some must think he was subverting nature."

"Not me. Otherwise, I wouldn't have agreed to be a part of his trials. I admired him for what he did. It wasn't an easy path to tread. I'm hopeful his work will continue. I'm a changed demon, thanks to him."

"And yet you're behind bars because the angels think you murdered Herbert," I said.

"You'll prove them wrong," he said. "I can tell you're clever. Besides, I have an alibi. I was with Abel Cross. He'll vouch for me."

Now we were getting to the interesting part. "Tell me about Abel."

Molvos smiled and nodded. "I've known him for years. You could say we're business partners.

Although he'd be more likely to say I'm his lackey. He's always joking around like that and pretending I get in his way."

"You've worked with Abel for a long time?"

"Years. We first met in an illegal gambling game. I'd snuck in, hoping to get my hands on some of the loot being gambled away. Abel was also there to take out someone causing his client problems."

"When you say take out, do you mean murder?"

"I don't question Abel about what he does for work. He doesn't like people knowing his business. All I know for sure was that he was there to erase a problem."

My heart lurched. "What do you know about his family?"

Molvos tilted his head. "I don't think he has a family. He's never talked about parents or a wife. Although he has a picture of a kid in his wallet. I've seen that a few times. And I sometimes see him hanging out with a younger woman. I figured she was his girlfriend."

"He can't have a girlfriend," I said. "He's a—" I stopped myself just before I blurted out he was married to my mom.

"Oh, I get it. Do you have a thing for the bad guys?" Molvos chuckled. "Isn't Abel a bit old for you, though? I mean, if you like the older guy that's fine, but I don't—"

"No! I don't have a thing for Abel." I wrinkled my nose. "Other than this woman you've seen him with, he never mentioned any children or relatives?"

"He's a man of few words," Molvos said. "He keeps his private life just that. You quickly learn not to ask questions when you deal with Abel. He's got a temper."

"What about his friends?"

"I consider myself a friend of his," Molvos said. "We hang out. We occasionally work jobs together, but he's more of a lone ranger type. Abel doesn't like getting close to people. He's a man of mystery."

"So, no family and not many friends." I tapped my fingers on the table top.

"It sounds like you have a personal interest in Abel. Has he messed with you in the past?" Molvos asked.

"No, nothing like that," I said. "But we have a history of sorts."

Molvos tilted his head from side to side. "It's funny, but in this light, you sort of look like him."

My eyes widened. If this demon could see the resemblance, why couldn't my dad?

"You're not some long-lost daughter, are you?" He chuckled.

"You wouldn't believe me if I told you." I forced myself to focus on the murder. "Abel will vouch for you during the time Herbert was killed?"

"I hope he will. We were in the bar having a drink."

"Why did the angels catch you near the crime scene?"

"I didn't know a murder had just happened around there. I had to leave the bar for a short while. I was late taking my medication."

"What medication? Are you sick?"

"It's a part of the cure Professor Winkler offered. I need to get regular top ups. You get a series of shots, and once a week, you have to take a potion to make sure things remain stable."

That didn't sound like a cure for demonism. It sounded more like Herbert had been repressing Molvos' behavior using magic. "What's going to happen now Herbert's dead? Will you still get access to the medication?"

He tapped his claws together. "I hope so. I've got a month's supply. After that, I'm not sure what will happen. Professor Winkler had an apprentice who helped during the trials. And he had a friend who lectures in Demonology. They were involved in the study. I'm sure they'll want to carry it on. I can get my medication from them."

Molvos seemed surprisingly happy that he no longer considered himself a demon. And he had an interest in keeping Herbert alive if he wanted to continue taking the medication that suppressed his urge to cause chaos.

"Do you believe me?" he asked. "Can I go now? I really am innocent."

"That's for the angels to decide."

"You'll put in a good word for me, though? I didn't kill Professor Winkler. I'm sad he's dead. I considered him a friend."

"I need to check your alibi before we do anything else." I stood and pushed my seat back.

He shrugged. "I can wait. It's not so bad being in here. The angels are nice to me. I would like to get out soon, though."

"I'll see what I can do about that." I left Molvos in the interview room and had just shut the door behind me, when sobbing drifted toward me.

I walked around the corner to see Herbert's mom talking to Sophie and dabbing at her eyes.

Sophie gestured me over. "This is the amazing demon catcher I was telling you about, Mrs. Winkler. She'll find out what happened to your son."

Mrs. Winkler grabbed my hand. "Please do everything you can to find the killer of my sweet boy. He was my only son. I relied on him for so much. I don't know what I'm going to do now he's gone."

I patted her shoulder. "We're making progress." Slow, confusing progress, but hopefully I was getting somewhere.

"Did that awful demon confess to the killing?" she asked.

"He's definitely talking," I said.

"Oh! That's good." Mrs. Winkler wobbled on her feet, and the color drained from her wrinkled face.

Sophie grabbed her by the shoulders. "Come sit down. I'll make you a hot drink, and you can rest for a while. Then I'll get someone to pick you up. You don't want to be alone at a difficult time like this."

"Yes, thank you. That's very kind of you. I just want to know what's going on. Everything is so confusing." Mrs. Winkler started to cry again as she was led away by Sophie.

Bandit strolled over, a half-eaten muffin in her hand. "How did it go?"

"Molvos sounds worryingly innocent," I said. "And he claims he doesn't want to be a demon. He was willingly involved in trials for Herbert's cure for demonism. I don't know what to make of him. There's no such thing as a good demon."

"Are you going to help that sweet old lady find out who killed her son?"

"She's got enough help." There were several angels around Mrs. Winkler, comforting her and offering her hankies and candy.

"You can't turn your back on that frail old sweetheart," Bandit said. "A strong gust of wind would knock her off her feet. She needs resolution. You can give her that."

"I never said I was giving up on finding the killer. I'll keep investigating, but I'm helping myself first."

"That's the motto I live by," Bandit said. "It never did me any harm."

"Apart from the time you were turned into a ginger cat because you irritated another magic user."

She scowled at me and dabbed a piece of muffin on my nose. "Let's forget about that embarrassing glitch in my past."

I shook my head. "We need to find my dad and question him. I have to make sure he's not guilty of murder before we do anything else."

"Then let's go find your long lost daddy and get him chatting."

Chapter 7

We'd been searching Puzzlewood for hours, and I hadn't been able to find my dad again. He'd gotten great at flying below the radar.

After a quick stop at a taco stand, I walked alongside Bandit, my feet aching and my heart thudding unhappily. I couldn't wrap my head around the fact my dad was so different, and he was mixing with a demon implicated in murder. Not only that, but he was also implicated in this murder. Given all the scenarios I'd imagined when I'd wondered what had happened to him when he'd vanished, this wasn't one of them.

"That weird weather is kicking off again," Bandit said. "Look at those black clouds."

I lifted my gaze to the rolling mass of angry clouds ahead of us. They weren't getting any closer. It looked like they were sitting over something. I slowed and took a look at a visitor map on the wall of one of the stores.

"Those clouds are hovering over the Puzzlewood cemetery," I said.

"Then we don't need to go there," Bandit said. "Nothing good comes out of clouds that color."

"I think we do," I said. "Dad loved spending time in the cemetery back home. He was the unofficial groundsman. He'd do a shift on demon patrol and spend the rest of the day tidying up the flower beds and pulling up weeds."

"You think your dad is causing that weird weather?"

"He used to influence weather, but he didn't practise those skills much, so his talent could be haphazard. He always said he left the tough stuff to his wife."

"That sounds wimpy to me."

I thumped her arm. "He wasn't a wimp. He was awesome. Mom's a Crypt witch. You don't get better than that. He wasn't afraid to have a strong, powerful witch by his side doing what she's supposed to do. Lesser men would have felt insecure, but Dad was always bragging about his wife and telling the world how amazing she was. It didn't make him any less of a man because he wasn't as powerful as her."

"You don't think he was hiding the fact that he hated not being the strong one in the family?"

"No, not for a second. Stop trying to stir trouble." I set off in the direction of the cemetery, not caring if Bandit followed me.

"Can your dad take out a demon?" She caught up with me.

"Only with help," I said. "He's a half-decent warlock. He was just a bit laid back when it came to using his magic."

"But he has the surname Crypt. I'm confused. How did that happen?"

"It's not complicated if you know your Crypt witch history. He married my mom. Anyone who marries into the family takes the Crypt surname. It's a tradition that goes back centuries. When you marry a Crypt witch, you become a Crypt by default."

"How very modern," Bandit said.

"That's the way it's always been. It's a kind of insurance policy. Whenever someone hears the surname, they know that person has the backing of dozens of powerful witches, who'll tear them apart if they mess with a member of the family."

"Even I might feel fear if you all ganged up on me."

"You'd be wise to. We'd kick your glittery behind into next year."

"That could be fun."

We left behind the stores and cute cottages and headed along a quiet lane. At the end of the lane was a set of large metal gates that stood open. The black clouds Bandit had spotted swirled over the cemetery.

I finished my taco, and we headed inside. It felt several degrees cooler as the clouds blotted out the weak sun that had struggled to make an appearance this morning.

The cemetery was neat and tidy, and the headstones were maintained by someone who had a serious aversion to weeds.

"I think we've found our man." Bandit tapped me on the shoulder. "Over there."

I turned in the direction she was pointing. My dad was perched on a large stone crypt, one leg hanging down, while his hand propped up his chin.

I looked around, but other than my dad, the place seemed deserted. I strode over, and although he didn't turn his head, his posture stiffened as he became aware of our presence.

"We need to talk," I said.

He glanced down at me and frowned. "You again. It seems you can't leave me alone."

"And I've got good reason not to," I said. "I'm helping the angels with the murder of Herbert Winkler."

"Good for you. I can't help you with that." He jumped off the crypt onto the ground and straightened. "What's a witch doing helping the angels, anyway?" His gaze flicked to Bandit, but he didn't say anything to her.

"I have an interest in this case," I said.

"Lucky you. You must have interesting hobbies if you like chasing murderers."

"You also have an interesting hobby if you like hanging out in cemeteries."

He lifted a shoulder. "I like being here. I can't explain it. Coming into a cemetery feels like home to me."

I sucked in a breath. Was he remembering the demon prison back home and the happy hours he'd spent there with his family?

He scrubbed a hand across his chin. "Why are you stalking me?"

I may as well get to the point. From the way Dad's gaze tracked around, he was hunting for an escape route. "Where were you two nights ago at eight o'clock in the evening?"

"Most likely at the bar where we first met," he said. "I go there when I've got free time, which is all the time right about now. The joy of working freelance."

"Were you with anybody?"

"Nope. I prefer to drink alone."

"What about the demon, Molvos?"

His eyes narrowed a fraction. "Never heard of him."

"Are you sure about that?" I asked. "He seems to know you."

"Then he's lying. Demons can't be trusted. You don't want to believe anything he tells you."

"You weren't with Molvos at the time of Herbert's murder?"

"That's about right." He looked around the cemetery again. "You've got the right guy in custody for that messy business."

"How can you be so sure if you don't know him? Were you there when he killed Herbert?"

He smirked at me. "No, I was in the bar, like I just told you."

"Can anyone support that alibi?"

"I doubt it. It's not a popular place. The tourists never come in, which is why I enjoy going there. Nobody asks any questions, the beer isn't terrible, and people mind their own business. You should take that advice. It might keep you out of trouble."

"Why would Molvos use your name as his alibi if you weren't going to stick up for him?" I asked.

My dad blew out a breath. "I have no idea. You'll have to ask him."

"I already have. He convinced me that he was with you."

"Then you've been deceived by a demon. It happens to the best of us. They can be sneaky. It's what being a demon is all about."

Dad was lying. He wasn't meeting my gaze and kept shifting around as if he was about to bolt. "What do you know about Herbert Winkler's work?"

"Not much. He was a loudmouth show off. Taking people's money and making false claims he couldn't back up."

"You didn't think much of him?"

"I guess you got me there. If what that guy reckoned is true, it'll mean big changes in the world of demons. That could mean less work for me. That's never good."

"You hunt demons for a living?" I asked.

"I hunt anything, so long as I get paid to do it."

"And if Herbert's demon cure is real, you'll be out of business?"

"There'll always be people who pay to get rid of problems in their lives," he said. "It might mean I have to work a bit harder. No one wants to do that."

"Did someone pay you to get rid of Herbert?" I asked. "Or maybe you decided to do it yourself to make sure you had enough money in your pocket."

My dad snorted a quiet laugh. "I'm not that motivated."

"It gives you a motive, though," I said.

"For murder? Not me. I don't know why you're stirring this up," he said. "The angels have Molvos. They'll charge him soon enough. Case closed."

"I'm not so sure they will," I said. "They're interested in you now."

He tipped his head back and sighed. "Okay, maybe I was in the bar with Molvos for most of that evening. The little sneak slipped out without paying the bar bill. Why should I cover his butt when he dropped me in it like that?"

"Because it could save you from a murder charge." I tugged on the ends of my hair, trying to keep my anger in check. He was being so unhelpful. "Dad, this is a big problem for you."

Bandit swiped me across the head with a wing, and I grimaced at my mistake.

"Dad? You've got me mixed up with someone else, kid." He grinned at me. "If you're looking for a sugar daddy, that ain't me. I'm a free man. I don't let anything tie me down."

The thought made me shudder. "I'm definitely not looking at you to be my sugar daddy," I said through gritted teeth.

"Good to know." He stepped away. "I've answered enough of your questions. You don't have any authority around here, and I'm all out of being friendly for the rest of the year."

I blocked his path. "I'm not done yet."

"I am. Get out of the way." His fingers flexed.

"No, you need to tell me about your involvement with Herbert. If you don't, the angels will come after you. I may not be able to arrest you, but they'll happily take you down."

"Sure they will. When they've filled in the right paperwork and triple-checked I'm free to arrest within their working hours." He stepped closer and glared down at me. "I wasn't involved with Herbert.

We didn't wallow in the same social circles. Now, I suggest you think carefully about your next move."

I sparked magic on my fingers, refusing to back down. "I suggest you do, too. An innocent person isn't going down for this murder."

"Molvos isn't innocent."

"But he's no killer."

The corner of his eye twitched. "You don't know that. Besides, he's a demon. They can't be trusted. What's one less demon on the loose?"

"That's not how I operate." Magic sparked and burned on my fingers as I held it in check, my pulse pounding.

My dad's lips pursed before he stepped back. "I don't fight girls. Not even ones with big mouths and a death wish."

"And I don't usually fight warlocks whose most impressive spell is conjuring a rain cloud."

His forehead wrinkled. "What are you talking about?"

Bandit cleared her throat. "Tempest is good at sensing another magic user's strength. She knows not to go up against me because I'd destroy her in a flat second. But you, you're no match for her."

"Huh! You don't say." My dad's expression sharpened. "I like a challenge. Maybe you don't know me as well as you think you do."

"You'd be surprised," I muttered. "I know all your moves."

His gaze ran over me. "It's weird. You remind me of someone. I keep getting this fuzzy kind of memory about a woman who looks like you. I don't think it's you, though."

I glanced at Bandit, and she gave a discreet shake of her head. I longed to tell him about his family and get him to remember. But I couldn't risk it. He could be under a curse or a suppression spell, so he literally couldn't remember his past. Would I damage him if I revealed the truth and shattered the illusion he'd been living under for so long?

"Forget it." He waved a hand in the air. "I see so many faces, they all blur into one."

"Is the memory you have good?" I asked.

He nodded slowly. "I'm not getting any bad vibes from it. Maybe it's a former girlfriend I'm remembering. I don't know. It's not important."

"But proving your innocence is," I said. "And I want to help do that."

His gaze instantly narrowed again. "Why? What's in it for you? I've got nothing to pay you with if that's your angle."

"I don't want -"

"Tempest is all about making sure justice is done," Bandit said. "She's a selfless individual, who's always looking out to right the wrongs in other people's lives."

I shot her a sideways glare. "Something like that. I do want to know who killed Herbert. I don't think it was Molvos, and I don't think it was you."

"You're a lousy judge of character if you think we're both innocent parties," my dad said. "You really don't want money?"

"Keep your cash. I have plenty of my own," I said.

"Is that so?"

"I know how to look after myself. My dad taught me that." I lifted my chin.

His mouth twisted before he nodded. "If you want to get me off the hook for this, you're welcome to take your best shot. I don't like the stain of murder on my record."

"Good." I exhaled a quiet breath. "Let's start with your alibi."

He lifted a hand. "I may not have been totally truthful."

"You were with Molvos?" I asked.

"I know him. I hire him sometimes to do the grunt work. I was in the bar with him that evening. We were having a few drinks and talking about making a move on our next job. But then he left."

"Leaving you with the bill?"

"Yeah, but then I snuck off, too. I was a little short. Besides, I had business to sort out. I'd have come back and paid what I owed, eventually. The barman knows me well enough to know I always settle my debts."

"What kind of business are we talking about? Was it linked to Herbert?"

He scrubbed at the back of his neck. "This is where it gets complicated. I was paid to get rid of a problem. That problem just happened to be named Herbert Winkler."

A gasp shot out before I could stop it. "You were going to kill him?"

"It was an option. Sometimes, I do a mind wipe. I give the person a blank slate, so they can start again and recreate themselves."

"You're not strong enough to do a mind wipe," I said.

My dad's lips thinned, and Bandit coughed into her hand.

"You don't know that's true. Even if it is, there are spells you can buy that do the job for you," my dad said, a curious look on his face. "I prefer that method. I'm not big on taking someone's life."

"But you have killed?" I almost didn't want to hear the answer.

"Now and again. When you're in a tight spot and that's the only thing left to do, you have to act to save yourself." He looked away and adjusted the collar of his T-shirt. "Anyway, I took this job to get Herbert Winkler out of the picture. I didn't ask why. And so long as I got the money, I didn't care."

"What happened?"

"Nothing happened. I'd been following him for a few days while he was touring with his new book. I heard he was coming to Puzzlewood for a break, which was perfect. It would be easier to get at Herbert when he didn't have adoring fans surrounding him. I checked out where they were staying and decided to make my move. But I didn't have to. Someone got there before I did. I figured it was Molvos."

"Molvos knew about this job?"

"He did. It was one of the easiest jobs I've ever had. I wouldn't have chosen the slash and murder route he took, but it meant I got paid to do nothing."

"Who paid you?"

My dad shook his head. "That's all you're getting from me. I don't ask why I'm paid to silence someone, and I don't know who's behind the job. It's all done anonymously. It's better for both parties. I take the money, do the work, and keep my head down."

I took a few seconds to process the information. My dad was connected to this murder, and he'd been planning on doing something bad to Herbert, but Molvos got there before he did? I still wasn't convinced it was Molvos, but he now had a motive and a hole in his alibi.

"You think that will clear my name? Get the angels off my back?" my dad asked.

"I can guarantee Tempest will clear your name. No matter what it takes," Bandit said.

"Don't be so sure about that," I said.

"You do what you have to, dark cherub," my dad said.

I took a step back, my heart racing. That was the nickname he'd given me years ago when I was struggling to control my spells and kept blasting out black jets of magic and setting things on fire. "Why... why did you call me that?"

He shrugged. "No idea. I'm out of here. See you around, kid."

I turned and watched him leave the cemetery, my palms clammy and my mind spinning so much I had to grab a headstone to stay upright.

He definitely would see me around. My dad was hiding inside that rough, unfriendly guy. And I planned to get him out and back home where he belonged.

Chapter 8

"Tell me again what it was like the first time you saw him." Aurora's face loomed on the snow globe in our motel room.

Wiggles was by her side, and they both jostled to share the space on the globe and stay in view.

I'd been talking to them for twenty minutes, giving an update on what had been going on in Puzzlewood.

"There's not much else to tell you. We've spoken. Things are going slowly. He's different. I keep telling you that."

"We're different too," she said. "That's not a bad thing."

"I'm definitely different," Wiggles said. "When your dad was last around, I was your every day, average dog. Now, I'm an awesome hellhound."

"You're not that awesome," Bandit said from her sprawled position on the bed.

"I'm way better than you," Wiggles said.

"Not according to Tempest," Bandit said. "She's thinking of replacing you. And guess who she's considering to take your spot."

"Don't listen to Bandit," I said. "Wiggles, you're irreplaceable."

"Tempest was having trouble remembering your name earlier today," Bandit said. "She called you wogglesock. Or was it wagstink?"

"I've been away for two days," I said. "Stop goading Wiggles."

"Yeah, stop goading me, or I'll come bite you," Wiggles said. "You're not forgetting about me, are you?"

"Of course not," I said. "But I am focused on Dad. It doesn't help that he's tied up in this murder."

"I spoke to Dazielle about that." Concern crossed Aurora's face. "She said she couldn't share much information, but a demon was involved in the murder of Professor Herbert Winkler."

"A demon who's also friends with our dad," I said. "They alibi for each other, but the alibis aren't great. And it doesn't help that Dad got paid by a mysterious person to make the Herbert Winkler problem disappear."

"I can't believe he's working as a bounty hunter," she said. "He used to love gardening. That's what he was great at. The cemetery hasn't been the same since he left."

"He still likes cemeteries," I said. "And his old memories are hiding, but there's work to do to get him to remember everything."

Aurora's smile slipped. "That's a temporary thing. You said yourself that he's starting to remember you."

"Not as such. He's recalling odd phrases and fuzzy memories. Whoever took away his memories did a good job."

Aurora worried her bottom lip with her teeth. "Does Frank have anything to say about this problem of memory loss?"

"Not a peep. I can feel him, but he's not getting involved." I almost wished he would. At least then, I'd know if there was any truth to the rumor he was behind Dad's disappearance.

"Be careful. You don't want to make him angry," Aurora said.

"I absolutely do. If he's behind this, I'm going to..." Actually, I wasn't sure what I'd do if it turned out Frank had forced Dad to leave. I could hardly kick him out.

"You must make Dad remember," Aurora said.

"I'm working on it. How are things at your end?"

She twirled a piece of hair around her fingers. "Things are tricky."

"You have told Mom and everyone else what's going on?"

"We finally did it this morning," she said. "At first, there was a horrible stunned silence. Then everyone started talking at once. It was awful. Mom cried and then laughed. I thought she was going to faint at one point. Auntie Queenie flapped around, trying to calm everyone down. Granny Dottie mainly drank brandy. The familiars ran out the back door because everyone was making so much noise. Then Mom wanted to know where you were, so she could visit and see Dad."

"No! We can't have Mom here. Not yet. Dad's also being tricky. I'd hate for her to meet him at the moment. What if he didn't remember her?" It had been like a gut punch when he hadn't recognized me. I wouldn't risk my mom experiencing the same thing.

"Maybe that's what he needs. A real blast from the past to jog his memories into place."

"Coming face-to-face with one of his daughters should have been a big enough blast," I said.

"Unless you aren't his favorite daughter," Bandit murmured.

"Shut up, Bandit," I said at the same time as Aurora.

Bandit lifted a hand. "I'm just saying."

"I looked straight at Dad, and he didn't even blink. There was no recognition on his face. There's some serious magic stopping him from remembering us, and that won't be easy to unpick. We have to make sure there's no long-lasting damage before we remove it."

Aurora was quiet for a few seconds. "You don't think he did kill that man, do you? You keep telling me that he's changed. What if he's turned dark?"

"He's definitely on the wrong side of magic law these days," I said. "I got him to open up a bit when we were in the cemetery. He let slip that he doesn't kill people unless he absolutely has to."

Aurora grimaced. "Maybe he absolutely had to kill Herbert."

"Herbert Winkler had a long line of people who wanted him dead, including most of the demons who don't want their abilities taken away with his cure."

"I've been researching Professor Winkler," Aurora said. "He's been working for decades on finding a way to remove a demon's power. I found reports of several death threats against him. There was even a previous attempt on his life."

"Which is good news. It makes it less likely that Dad was involved."

"It's not just demons you have to consider as suspects," Aurora said. "There are plenty of other magic users who make use of demons to carry out their dark wishes. Is there anyone else in Puzzlewood who'd benefit from Herbert's death?"

"That's what I need to find out," I said. "I can't believe Dad had anything to do with this. And the demon in the angels' custody doesn't strike me as a killer. He claimed to be a fan of Herbert's and happily underwent the treatment to have his demon power removed."

"Then you need to get asking around," Aurora said. "And you need to hurry up and get our dad back home. I can only contain the situation here for so long. Mom's constantly questioning me and trying to find out where you are. You know I'm terrible at keeping secrets."

"You have to keep this one," I said. "She can't come here. It would break her heart to see Dad right now."

"I wish I could be there with you," she said. "I want to help."

"Me too," Wiggles said. "I'd solve this mystery for you. Much quicker than that fairy could."

"You keep telling yourself that, puppy," Bandit said. "I'm Tempest's new indispensable sidekick from now on."

"Ignore Bandit," I said. "You're both helping me by researching Herbert and keeping the family from going crazy. I'll get in touch soon with another update."

We said our goodbyes, and I shut off the snow globe.

"You aren't helping by goading Wiggles," I said to Bandit.

"But it's so much fun to goad him. The look on his furry little face is to die for."

"It's not fair. He wants to be here."

"Pah! He deserves it. He was mean to me when I was a sick cat."

I stood and rolled my shoulders. "Let's get out of here and head to Angel Force before they close for the evening. There are people we need to talk to."

"People who may have wanted Herbert dead?"

"That's what I'm thinking."

"Fine by me." Bandit rolled off the bed in a single fluid movement. "So long as there's food involved soon. I'm getting hungry."

"You're worse than Wiggles," I said.

"That's not possible."

We headed out of the motel and back to the Angel Force office.

After filling in the appropriate authorization form to get through and see Sophie, we were ushered through the back, with promises of tea and cookies.

Sophie raised a hand and smiled as I entered her office. "Have you made progress since your interview with Molvos?"

I sat in a seat, and Bandit lounged by the door. "I hate to burst your happy bubble, but I'm not certain it was him."

"Oh! That makes things awkward." Sophie's pretty face scrunched up. "Should we release him?"

"Not yet. He's not in the clear. I've spoken to Abel. I'm also not convinced he's your killer."

"This is terrible news. I was so certain they were involved." Her hands fluttered across her desk. "What should we do next?"

"I'm interested in the people Herbert was staying with. I'm assuming they haven't left town."

"That's right. You're welcome to talk to them," she said. "They're still in Puzzlewood."

"Remind me who they are."

"Herbert traveled with his business partner, Saul, his apprentice, Brendan, his best friend Jeremiah, and his former girlfriend, Virginia. Jeremiah lectures in demonology and helped with the talks Herbert gave. Virginia, the former girlfriend, now assists with the tour activities."

"I'd like to speak to all of them," I said. "I want to find out more about who he was close to. Maybe one of them noticed something suspicious that evening."

"Like Molvos lurking around waiting to strike?"

"Or someone lurking around," I said. "Abel and Molvos confirmed they were with each other around the time of the murder."

"That doesn't put them in the clear," Sophie said. "And Molvos was seen close by the crime scene. I wish they had done it. It would make this investigation so much easier. If we introduce new suspects, it'll add to the paperwork."

I arched an eyebrow. "A little extra paperwork to find a killer can't be a bad thing."

Sophie's cheeks flushed. "You're right. I'm being selfish. Paperwork never does anyone any harm. And I have the perfect idea. I've invited Saul to dinner tonight. You can start with him. He's been friends with Herbert for years."

"Did someone say dinner?" Bandit strode over to the desk. "We should definitely go to dinner together."

"Then it's agreed," Sophie said. "Do you have something nice to wear?"

I tilted my head. "For dinner? We have to dress up?"

"You do. We're having the Angel Appreciation Society dinner tonight at the gala hall."

I sat forward in my seat. "I figured this was dinner at your apartment."

"Oh, no. This is an annual event held in Puzzlewood. There'll be angels coming from all over to celebrate the successes and hard work of Angel Force."

"That doesn't sound like a good place to talk to Saul," I said. Plus, being surrounded by sparkly, cheerful angels all night would give me a thumping headache.

"Will there be free food?" Bandit asked.

"Yes, plenty of free food," Sophie said. "It's a banquet. We have seven courses. And that's before we get to the desserts."

"We're in," Bandit said.

I groaned before nodding. If it meant I got access to Saul, I'd endure a room full of super positive angels for the night.

"I'm so pleased." Sophie stood and gestured us to follow her. "Now, about your outfits..."

Chapter 9

"Well, well, well. Don't you scrub up nicely." Bandit grabbed my arm and twirled me around the second I stepped out of the bathroom in our motel room.

"I feel ridiculous." The dress code for the angels' dinner was all white. What a shocker. Sophie had rented me a floor length white gown with spaghetti straps and crystal detail around the neckline. It swept to the floor and skimmed my shoes.

"You should wear white more often," Bandit said. "It suits you."

"I'll stick to black. It hides the stains." My gaze ran over her. Although Bandit was still a sparkly green, she'd covered herself in an iridescent creamy white glitter that made her shine. The effect was spectacular. She looked like a giant winter angel, just with sharp teeth.

"We need to get a move on, or we'll be late for the opening of the banquet." Bandit yanked me out of the motel room. "I'm not missing a single one of those courses."

We headed outside, and I spotted several angels striding toward the large hall where the dinner was being held. Excited chatter filled the air, and white angel feathers drifted around us.

We were stopped at the entrance of the hall by a large angel with a clipboard. "Names, please."

"I'm Bandit, and this is Tempest Crypt. We're special guests of Sophie," Bandit said.

"Welcome to the event. Have a lovely evening." The angel smiled as she ticked our names off and gestured us inside.

There was so much white in the hall, I was dazzled. Classical music played in the background, and three giant chandeliers cast a warm glow around the large reception foyer.

"I can smell the amazing food." Bandit fluttered her wings, almost poking a passing angel in the face.

"Remember what we're here for. This is about questioning Saul, not stuffing our faces."

"We can do both. You question and I'll stuff." Bandit grabbed two glasses of something sparkly off a tray. She drank them both.

I looked around, hoping to catch a glimpse of Sophie, so she could steer us toward Saul.

"We should find our seats," Bandit said. "That way, we can be ready when the food arrives. I'll also be able to grab extra portions if they've made too much. We don't want anything to go to waste."

I followed her through the crowd of angels, holding up my hem to avoid tripping. I was used to jeans and sweatpants, not flouncy skirts. At least I'd convinced Sophie that I didn't need heels and sported an already slightly scuffed pair of white ballet pumps covered in glittering stones.

"Here's the table plan." Bandit stopped in front of a board and ran a finger over it. "Here we are. Table number six. And look! You're sitting next to Saul."

"Tempest, I'm so glad you could make it."

I turned and saw Sophie approaching us. She was dressed in a white gown with her arms bare. Artificial flowers and lace covered the skirt, and two large white feathers poked out of her hair.

"We wouldn't miss this," Bandit said. "When's the food being served?"

"Not long now," Sophie said. "I've shuffled people around and managed to get Saul on your table. That'll give you a chance to chat to him."

"That's great. Thanks," I said. "Is anyone else from Herbert's touring party here?"

"Not tonight. This is an exclusive event. Herbert was originally supposed to come, so I gave Saul his ticket and suggested it might be a nice way to honor his friend's memory by attending."

"That's sneaky for an angel," Bandit said.

"We're here to get justice for Herbert. I'm being creative." Sophie's round cheeks grew pink. "I didn't break any rules."

"You absolutely didn't," I said. "This is perfect."

"And if you don't get anywhere with Saul, we can arrange to see the others tomorrow."

"That would work for me," I said. Although I was hoping to do some sneaky surveillance on my dad and see how he spent his time.

Bandit tugged on my arm. "They're bringing out platters of food. We should take our seats."

Sophie smiled. "Enjoy the evening. I won't be able to spend much time with you. I'm entertaining several special guests. We have the head of the award ceremony at my table. She demands my full attention."

"Don't worry. We can entertain ourselves," I said.

Bandit yanked me into the dining hall and found our allocated table. "Wiggles will be so jealous that he's missing this. I'm going to remember everything about the food, so I can describe it to him in great detail."

"Don't be mean," I said. I was missing that stinky hellhound. I couldn't wait to get back to Willow Tree Falls and hang out with him. And I'd make it up to him that he missed out on this dinner with a huge box of his favorite doughnuts.

The rest of the diners made their way into the hall, and soon, three hundred people were settled around the tables. Although the seat next to me, where Saul was supposed to be, remained empty.

The waiters came out and served the first course.

Bandit stared at the small plate of rock shrimp in front of her. "It's not very big."

"Remember, there are seven courses, plus dessert," I whispered. "You don't want to get full too quickly."

"I definitely won't get full on this." She scooped up the three shrimp and ate them in one bite. She grabbed mine and ate that as well.

"I may have wanted that," I muttered.

"As you said, loads more to come. And you don't want to eat too much. That dress is already on the tight side."

I glowered at her but turned as the seat next to me was pulled out.

"My apologies for being late. I got caught up in a fascinating discussion with an angel over the different levels of heaven." He held out his hand. "I'm Saul Connelly."

I smiled. Just the man I wanted to see. "Tempest Crypt."

He introduced himself to the rest of the diners at the table as he settled in his seat.

"This is quite an event. The angels certainly know how to look after people," he said.

"It's my first formal angel dinner," I said. "It's all very white."

He chuckled. "Yes, I suppose it is." Saul was in his mid-forties, with black hair and dark brown eyes. He wore a sharp suit that looked tailored, and his hair was slicked back off his face.

"Sophie told me you stepped in after the unfortunate incident with Herbert," I said, leaning close, so the other diners couldn't overhear.

"Ah. Yes. She thought it was the right thing to do. It was a terrible business. I'm still in shock. I believe the angels are making progress, though." He looked my way and lifted his chin. "Weren't you with the angels the other day at their office?"

"That's right. I'm helping with the investigation."

His gaze ran over me. "You're some kind of special investigator?"

"Something like that. I have a talent when it comes to demons."

"How interesting. Herbert would have loved to have spoken to you. He was so close to fulfilling his ambition of offering a cure. He always loved to speak to people who had special insight into the dark world of demons."

"He hadn't gotten there yet?"

"Almost. The last trial was promising. Herbert was about to announce a huge breakthrough. His new book details the work done to date and the next chapter in the cure. He'd have done it. He was a great man."

"It sounds like you were close."

"We'd worked together for fifteen years. We both have a fascination with demons."

"Why the interest?" I nodded at the server as she removed my plate.

Saul arched an eyebrow. "I have an ability to sense what other people are thinking."

"You're empathic?"

"Only mildly. And it's more of a psychic link I make than a talent for enhanced empathy. I've been around demons long enough to know that most of their thoughts revolve around chaos and destruction. There's no good in a demon."

"That's an obvious conclusion to come to," I said. "That's how it's always been. You have the good and bad. We have angels and demons, and they balance each other out."

"True enough. But I've heard so many concerning thoughts from demons that I had to do something to help minimize the risk to others. Herbert was already working on his cure when we met. We shared the same passion for ridding the world of darkness."

"I imagine a lot of demons weren't happy about that."

He took a sip from his wine glass. "We had our problems. And our worst fears came true when that disgusting little demon murdered Herbert."

"You sound certain it was Molvos who killed Herbert."

"I should be. I saw him fleeing the scene of the crime."

"Did you see him attack Herbert?"

"No, nothing like that. I was heading toward the house we'd rented. I turned the corner, and Molvos slammed into me. He seemed panicked. I told him to be careful, but he didn't slow down. He simply raced away and then ran straight into an angel."

"You saw him come out of the house?"

"As good as. There are only three houses along the lane. And when I got there, the front door was open. Molvos must have been in a hurry to get away before anyone spotted him."

"And you told the angels this?" I asked. "You didn't actually see Molvos kill Herbert?"

"I told them everything I just told you. They seemed happy with the information. It was enough evidence for them to arrest Molvos. I just wish he'd confess. It would make this sad business easier to bear. I lost a good friend. And the world has lost an incredibly intelligent man who was about to change everything."

That wasn't great evidence to implicate Molvos in Herbert's murder. "Did you go into the house and discover what happened to Herbert?"

He cleared his throat before nodding. "It was horrifying."

Saul had made some big assumptions about what had happened. He was also demonstrating his prejudice against demons. Although he had a right to be prejudiced. Demons were chaos makers. Whenever there was trouble, a demon was usually involved.

But it was a leap to believe that, because he'd bumped into Molvos near the house Herbert had been murdered in, he was the killer. The case against Molvos grew flimsier with each person I talked to.

I took a breath as the second course was served.

"Tortilla soup with chicken and avocado," the waiter announced.

I wasn't a big soup fan, so pushed my dish over to Bandit before she grabbed it. I was more interested in talking than eating.

"I'm not surprised Molvos did this," Saul said.

"Why do you say that?"

"As I said, Herbert was a great man. But sometimes, his passion to find a cure led to him being inventive when it came to finding test subjects." Saul glanced around at the other diners.

"I thought Molvos was a willing test subject," I said. "He told me he had no problem with Herbert and was happy to take the cure."

Saul inclined his head before sighing. "He may be happy now."

"But not to begin with?"

"It wasn't easy to find demons willing to be in a trial that removed their powers. When we first started working together, we used a private security firm to locate criminals for our experiments."

My mouth dropped open as I stared at him. "You forced demons to be test subjects?"

"I know it doesn't sound ideal, but they were given reduced sentences in return for being involved. Some even received financial compensation. It was the only way we could get the trials off the ground. And when we ran short of test subjects from that particular source, Herbert found other ways to gather them. Ways I didn't approve of."

"Ways that don't sound legal," I said.

Saul scratched his nose. "You must understand, his work was the most important thing to him."

"And demons make the world a dangerous and unstable place. A few less demons around is only a good thing." My eyes narrowed. "You must have known what he was doing."

Saul pressed his lips together. "Herbert took in demons who had no home and little to live for. He gave them a chance at something different."

That sounded like a whitewash to me. "He kidnapped demons who were vulnerable and forced them into his experiments."

"Kidnapping is the wrong word. And no demon is ever really vulnerable." Saul shook out his napkin. "And when they realized they were in a safe place, fed regularly, and looked after, most were happy to take part in the trials. Even Molvos softened toward the end."

"But he wasn't always compliant?"

"I always wondered about him. I'd catch brief glimpses of his thoughts. They were never positive when it came to Herbert." He shook his head. "We should have been more careful. Herbert was so convinced the demons would side with him in the end and see this was the right path to take."

Either Saul was lying or Molvos was. Molvos had convinced me when he'd said he didn't want his demon powers. Had I been duped by him?

"What will happen to Herbert's plans now he's gone?" I asked.

"That's an excellent question. I've discussed this at length with the others. We've decided, in Herbert's memory, to complete the lecture tour, finish his research, and publish it. The profits from the book will go into a foundation in his name. It'll ensure his work can continue. The book will be a bestseller if pre-release numbers continue the way they are. We'll be able to complete the research and produce the cure Herbert always wanted."

This wasn't a bad motive for murder. If this demon cure worked, it would make Saul and anyone else involved very wealthy.

"Will you take over Herbert speaking engagements?" I asked.

"No, public speaking isn't my area of expertise. I was always the planner and investor in Herbert's project. I made sure we had enough financial security to continue his work. I'll head up the work of the foundation. Jeremiah will take over as the lead speaker. I may get Herbert's apprentice, Brendan, to undertake some smaller events. They're both experts in demonology. Jeremiah lectures on the subject and goes around the world giving presentations. He'll be a popular draw. The tour won't suffer."

Neither would the bottom line. Saul had a lot to gain from Herbert being dead. He could set up this foundation, rake in the profits, possibly skimming some off the top to pay himself a generous salary, and bask in the glory as other people finished Herbert's work.

"I'm sure the angels have already asked, but where were you just before Herbert died? You said you were walking back to the house."

He arched an eyebrow but nodded. "That's right. I'd been with Brendan, running over the schedule. We'd planned to stay in Puzzlewood for a few days to give Herbert a rest. He pushed himself so hard during these tours."

That would be an easy enough alibi to check. "When you bumped into Molvos, did you see any injuries on him or any sign of a struggle?"

"It all happened so fast, but it was simple to put it all together when I discovered Herbert. I assumed this case would be simple to solve. What kind of expertise did you say you have?"

"Mainly demon related." I glanced at Bandit, who was licking her bowl clean. "Molvos is in custody, but we need to be thorough. The angels want to make sure the right individual is charged."

"I heard Molvos was being difficult," Saul said.

"We're simply covering all the bases. Can you think of anyone else who had a problem with Herbert?"

"A problem big enough to kill him?"

I nodded before grabbing the plate of food placed in front of me by the server. I was getting hungry, and Bandit wasn't having all my courses.

"Well, I had concerns about Virginia," Saul said. "I was surprised when Herbert insisted she come on the tour with us."

"Wasn't she his assistant?"

"And former girlfriend. I'm worried about her mental stability. Her thoughts are frantic and unfocused. Not that she isn't clever. Virginia has her own interest in demonology. But she was obsessed with Herbert, even though they were no longer together."

"Did Herbert realize she still had feelings for him?"

"No, and she'd have needed to stand in front of him with a large sign declaring her affections for him to notice. Herbert was only interested in his work. He brought her along because he felt sorry for her. She seemed directionless after they separated. They were together for several years. Herbert earned a lot of money in a short space of time, and he was cautious about who he had around him. He didn't want to be used for his wealth. He trusted Virginia."

"I imagine, if the cure takes off, that wealth will only grow."

"Correct. We were working out the fine details of the distribution for the cure just before he died. Herbert was about to become a billionaire."

"Wow! That's a lot of money."

"And Virginia was aware of that potential fortune. I fear Herbert let her see too much. When they first split, she used to follow him around. It was a bit pathetic. I wondered how healthy her obsession was. I even mentioned it to Herbert, but he dismissed my concerns. He said she'd always have a place in his heart, but now wasn't the right time for them. He was focused on his work. I think she became jealous of that. She didn't like playing second fiddle to his obsession to find a demon cure."

"What's Virginia doing this evening?" I asked.

"Most likely holed up in her room researching something. During the day, she's been spending her free time in the library or at the bookstore. That's one thing I will say about her; she has a sharp mind. But the time I've spent with her since Herbert died has only made my concerns about her escalate. She's not thinking clearly."

"She must be upset. Maybe that's why her thoughts are so murky."

"Yes, perhaps it's that." His smile looked strained. "Anyway, I've been hogging your attention ever since I sat down. Please, enjoy the rest of your meal before your companion eats it all."

I glanced at my plate. Most of the ravioli I'd been looking forward to was gone. Only the green salad remained untouched.

I nudged Bandit. "Keep your sparkling fingers off my food."

Her eyes widened in mock innocence. "It wasn't me."

"Sure it wasn't." I stabbed a few pieces of rocket as I mulled over the conversation I'd just had. Saul was super confident about his role in Herbert's empire, and if his plans rolled out as he anticipated, he'd soon be a wealthy man.

However, there was also the obsessive ex-girlfriend in the background. Both Virginia and Saul had the label of potential killers firmly on their foreheads.

This case wasn't over yet. There were tangible suspects out there. Suspects with better motives than my dad or Molvos. I needed to keep digging.

Chapter 10

"Last night was brilliant." Bandit strolled along beside me the next morning. "The food was out of this world. And boy, can those angels dance."

"You didn't give them much choice but to dance," I said. "You'd grab anyone close at hand and spin them around the floor."

"They loved it," Bandit said. "Only one angel screamed when I threw her in the air."

I chuckled as I shook my head. We'd just had breakfast at the motel and were on our way to find Virginia.

I'd updated Bandit about my conversation with Saul the previous evening. She was in agreement that they both needed to be on the suspect list for Herbert's murder.

After a quick look around the bookstore for Virginia, we headed to the Puzzlewood library.

"Hey, they've got some Grimm's Fairy Tale comics. I loved those as a kid." Bandit bounded over to the comic section.

"Please, no talking," a small wood elf said from behind her desk. "This is the silent zone." She pointed to a sign above her head.

"Sorry," I whispered. "We're looking for the demonology section."

"Third floor." She pressed her fingers to her lips and raised her eyebrows.

I lifted a hand as an apology before catching hold of Bandit's arm and hurrying away from the fierce glare of the tiny librarian.

We headed up the stairs to the third floor. It was still early, so there weren't many people in the library.

"There's something magical about a room full of books," Bandit said.

"I didn't take you for a reader."

"Why not? All that learning and knowledge jammed into the pages. I have centuries of reading behind me."

"Mainly comics?"

"Comics feature heavily in my reading preferences. There's a lot to be learned from a good comic. You can guarantee an epic battle between good and evil and characters forced to make life-altering decisions. You can't go wrong with a good comic."

We walked along the book stacks, searching for Virginia.

"One second. I want to check out the section on dinosaurs." Bandit darted along the book stacks.

"We're not here to check out books," I whispered. "Keep focused."

"You focus. I'll grab some books to read. I should get a library card. I can borrow these while I'm here." Bandit glanced my way. "Here's an interesting fact about dinosaurs. They didn't read. Do you think that's why they went extinct?" She waggled a book in my face.

I waved her away as I continued my search for Virginia.

Bandit swooped past me on her wings, her arms loaded with books.

"No magic use in the library." The librarian who'd been downstairs appeared in front of us in a flash of light.

"Um, didn't you just use magic to appear?" I asked.

She jabbed a finger at me. "I'm the head librarian. I have written permission to use magic. However, visitors to this library may not use magic. It disturbs the magical book section."

Bandit's eyes widened. "There's a magical book section. Point me in the right direction, librarian."

"Shush. And stop shedding glitter everywhere." The librarian scrubbed her foot through a clump of Bandit's glitter. "If you keep flying around, the books will join you. No more magic use."

"Flying isn't technically magic if you're a fairy," Bandit said.

"Don't test my patience," the librarian said. "I'm watching you." She blinked out of sight.

"That is one scary little librarian," Bandit said.

"Then it's best you listen to her," I said. "Stop messing with the books."

We rounded the corner, and Bandit stopped dead, a reverential sigh escaping her lips.

"It's like all my dreams have come true." She shoved her books into my hands before marching over to a glass fronted room full of children's magical games.

"No! You're not going in there." I hurried over to join her. "Read the sign. You need to be under four foot tall and less than twelve years old to go in the children's magic area."

"There's no one around," Bandit said. "And there are no children in there. Just five minutes with the magic bubbles."

"No. Quit messing around."

Her hand went to the door. "Two minutes."

"Not even two seconds."

"Cover for me. I'm going in." Bandit shoved open the door. She ran to the bubble machine, grabbed hold of it, and sent a cascade of bubbles across the room. The bubbles shimmered in the air before popping, and candy fell out of them.

Bandit raced around laughing as she scooped up the candy.

There was a flash beside me, and the librarian appeared again. Her eyes narrowed. "I warned that fairy. I told her no more trouble."

"She's easily distracted," I said. "She doesn't get out much."

The librarian scowled at me as she pushed open the door, pulled a folded piece of paper out of her pocket, and slung it in the air. It expanded into a huge net, covering Bandit and pinning her to the ground.

I looked on in amazement. This librarian had some impressive powers if she could so easily trap Bandit.

Bandit's mouth opened, but no sound came out. It looked like she was frozen.

"You had your warning." The librarian stood over Bandit. She gathered up the edges of the net and tied them together, trapping Bandit inside.

"What have you done to her?" I stood to one side as the librarian dragged Bandit behind her as if she weighed no more than a couple of books.

"She's immobilized. These books have power. It doesn't do to have chaotic magic users around them."

"Is she okay?" I prodded a frozen Bandit with the toe of my boot.

"She hasn't been hurt, just stunned." The librarian moved away, pulling Bandit behind her with ease.

"Where are you taking her?"

"You can collect your friend from the reception desk when you're ready to leave. And neither of you is welcome back." She turned and stalked away.

I needed one of those nets. It would be perfect for bringing down demons.

I placed the books down. Bandit would be fine for half an hour, and I needed to find Virginia before the librarian came back for me.

I found her sitting at a desk in one corner right at the back of the library. Her head was down, her long dark hair covering her face as she read a book.

"Are you Virginia Lupin?" I asked.

She lifted her head and blinked purple eyes at me. "That's right. Oh, I know you. You were with the angels the other day."

"That's right. I'm Tempest. I'm helping them investigate Herbert's murder. I have some questions for you. It could help us figure out what happened to him."

She glanced down at her book before closing it and nodding. "Of course."

"There's some doubt surrounding who was involved in his death." I settled in the seat opposite her.

Her forehead furrowed. "It was Molvos. Everyone knows it was him."

"I've spoken to Saul and Molvos about the events leading up to Herbert's death. There are inconsistencies in their statements. And there's no conclusive evidence that Molvos killed Herbert."

"And you think Saul or Molvos is lying?" She splayed her hands out. "The demon is lying. It has to be him."

"Possibly. Tell me about your relationship with Herbert."

She brushed her hair off her face. "I cared for him very much."

"You were intimate?"

Her cheeks grew pink. "For a short time."

"He was older than you, wasn't he?"

"There was an almost twenty year age gap. It didn't bother me. My mom always said I have an old soul, and I've always preferred mature men. Our relationship changed toward the end. I came to see him as a father figure rather than a husband. Not that we were married. I eventually realized that his one true love was his work."

"That must have been difficult to accept, coming second place to his research."

"I wasn't happy, but we'd been drifting for some time before it ended."

"Did you break things off with him, or was it the other way around?"

"It just sort of fizzled out. We stopped going on dates and began working together like colleagues. The spark died. One day, I simply said to him, 'It's over, isn't it?' He agreed. It wasn't difficult, but I was sad it didn't work out."

"You've joined him on this book tour, though," I said. "Isn't that a bit odd?"

"Not really. I took on the role of Herbert's personal assistant. He was so forgetful about the practical things. Sometimes, he'd get so involved in his research that he'd forget the most basic things. There were even occasions when he wore the same clothes for days because he didn't care. He was focused only on his research. I stepped in and took over those areas he wasn't so good at. Pretty soon, that spilled over into helping with the business. He told me he needed me by his side or he'd fall apart. I guess I was flattered. It's nice to be needed."

"You seem certain Molvos was involved in Herbert's death."

"I'm certain the angels have the right demon. He's not to be trusted." She leaned across the desk. "The night we arrived in Puzzlewood, I saw a demon outside the house."

"What was it doing?"

"Watching the house."

"Did you report this to the angels?"

"I wasn't planning to, but that night, I was getting ready for bed when someone tried to break in through my window."

"The same demon?"

"I only caught a glimpse, but there were definitely scales. I screamed, and Herbert came to my room. The demon must have been startled and fled."

That sounded very unlike a demon to me. They didn't startle easily. If they got caught doing something they shouldn't, their first instinct was to go into attack mode. "What did the angels do when you reported the attempted break in?"

"They came and looked around but didn't find anything. They told us to keep the windows and doors locked and reassured us that Puzzlewood was safe." Virginia nodded slowly. "I think it was Molvos trying to get in and kill Herbert."

"But you didn't get a good look at the wannabe burglar?"

"No, but it makes sense it was him. Molvos is dangerous. And he's involved with dangerous individuals."

"Can you give me any names of these dangerous individuals?"

"I can give you one. Abel Cross. That man brings nothing but trouble with him."

My heart gave an unhappy thump. "How do you know Abel?"

Her nose wrinkled. "He was paid to get rid of a demon bothering my hometown about five years ago. It's only a small place, and we were struggling to manage the demon as he became more demanding. Someone suggested we get professional help. Abel was brought in. He wasn't cheap, but he assured us he could deal with the matter discreetly. He was there two weeks, and the place was in chaos when he left."

"Did he get rid of your demon problem?"

"Eventually, but he damaged several buildings, and magic users were injured. He was supposed to round up the demon and that would be an end to the trouble. The place hasn't felt the same since he visited. The world would be a much better place if Abel Cross was behind bars, just like Molvos. They're in this together."

"Actually, I have spoken to both of them." I tapped my finger on her book, keeping my anger in check. "And you know the saying, never judge a book by its cover. Maybe Abel isn't all bad. The same could go for Molvos."

She sniffed and shook her head. "I know those types. I've been working with Herbert for years. The demons in the trials were always unstable and dangerous. Some magic users simply have no goodness in them. That was the case with Molvos until he got his cure, and it definitely applies to Abel. I can't imagine what turned that warlock so dark."

"Maybe he suffered a loss. That can change a person." I spoke through gritted teeth.

"Well, whatever happened to him, he has my pity."

"I suspect he doesn't need it," I said. "Where were you when Herbert was murdered?"

She jerked back in her seat. "You can't think I was involved in his death. I loved him."

"So you won't mind telling me your alibi if you weren't involved."

Her gaze narrowed. "I suppose not. The angels know I was alone that evening. I was here, reading.

It's not a great alibi, but it's what I often do. It's not unusual for me to stay late in a place like this. I like the quiet." She shifted in her seat and glanced down at her hands. "The angels have it right. Molvos killed Herbert. I don't know why they haven't charged him. Then everyone can move on."

"People can move on soon enough, once the right person has been found." I pushed my chair back. I'd heard enough from Virginia, but I wasn't removing her from the suspect list. She could be angry about her failed relationship with Herbert. Maybe she wanted to keep things going, but he turned her down. And she had no alibi. Being alone in the library wasn't helpful.

"I hope you can help the angels to clear this up," she said. "I won't feel safe until they do."

"It won't be long now." I stalked down the stairs and back to the reception desk.

The librarian was there. Her glare suggested she wasn't pleased to see me.

"Where's Bandit?" I asked.

"Your misbehaving fairy has been contained in the lost and found room. Wait here. I'll bring her out." The librarian vanished and returned a few seconds later with Bandit still in the net. She touched the corner of the net, and it shrunk down to a tiny size before she placed it in her pocket.

Bandit rolled on the floor for a few seconds before springing to her feet and fluttering her wings, glitter cascading everywhere. "What just happened? Did that—"

"Not now." I grabbed her arm and hustled her out of the library. I didn't want to feel the wrath of that librarian pointed in my direction.

Bandit glared over her shoulder. "I need to teach that evil creature a lesson."

"Plan your revenge later. I just spoke to Virginia."

Bandit grumbled under her breath as she followed me. "And?"

"She was quick to point a finger at Molvos and my dad."

"Does she have any proof?"

"No, but she has a lot of negativity when it comes to demons. She's convinced Molvos did it."

"And her alibi?"

"It doesn't exist." I pushed open the main library door and walked out into the cool air. "Virginia could be good for this murder. No alibi, jealous ex, hates demons. She could have set Molvos up."

"Saul also needs to stay on the list," Bandit said. "He was way too smug for my liking. Maybe they're in on this together."

I nodded. "And there are more people to question before we get to the bottom of this. Let's keep looking."

"Did you bring my books?"

"Nope. And you're banned from the library."

"But... the comics. I did nothing wrong. That librarian must have a problem with fairies."

"You did a lot wrong. Murder first. Everything else must wait."

Chapter 11

"That's where we've gotten so far. This murder isn't as simple as the angels think." I lounged on the bed back in our motel, talking to Aurora and Wiggles via the snow globe.

"I still think your latest idea is a bad one." Bandit hurled a pillow at me.

"What's got her wings all twisted?" Wiggles asked.

"There's a lecture tonight. It was arranged so Herbert could talk about his new book," I said. "Sophie told me earlier that Saul and Jeremiah will be speaking instead."

"Which means we're going to a boring lecture," Bandit said. "There'll be no fun to be had listening to some stuffed shirts waffling on about science. And I bet they don't even serve food."

"You can take snacks. It may not be fun, but everyone we need to talk to will be there. Saul and Jeremiah are speaking, and I imagine Virginia and Brendan will put in an appearance in their supporting roles. They're who we need to focus on. If we find the weak link in the group, the chances are we'll discover the killer."

"Um, that all sounds great." The way Aurora kept glancing away from the snow globe suggested there was a problem.

"Is something wrong?" I said.

"I've been meaning to say," Aurora said, "we're not alone."

"Who else is there?"

She stepped backward, and her face disappeared. It was swiftly replaced by my mom's. Oh, crud. The concern on her face hit me right in the gut and made me queasy.

"Hey, Mom. How's it going?"

She let out a sigh. "Tempest, I wish you hadn't kept this from us. Everyone's so worried."

"I'm sure Aurora explained why I didn't say anything," I said. "And I made her keep quiet, so don't blame her. Things here aren't straightforward. I wanted to get everything sorted before telling you what was going on."

"And where is here?"

I bit my lip and shook my head. "It's best you don't know for now. I promise I'll explain everything when I get back."

She was silent for several seconds. "Will you be coming back alone?"

I glanced at Bandit. "I'm not sure. Hopefully, not."

Mom blinked several times. "And you've really found him?"

I couldn't stop a grin surfacing. "I have."

"Where has he been all these years? What has he told you?"

"I'm not sure of all the details. Dad moves around a lot because of his work."

"What kind of work is he doing?" She shook her head. "No, that's not important. Has he told you why he left?"

"Not yet. We're working through a few things." I needed to keep this conversation vague. I couldn't let anyone get too excited until I'd figured out how to get Dad home where he belonged and with his old memories back.

"Aurora told me he seems... different. Wasn't he happy to see you?"

"It's not that. We're taking it slowly."

"He must have been delighted to have you back in his life," she said.

"I'm sure deep down he was. The time away from us has changed him." I wasn't ready to tell her that he had no memories of his family. It would hurt her too much. I was determined to find a way to get Dad to remember who he was and everything he'd left behind in Willow Tree Falls.

"Perhaps if I see him, talk to him," she said, "it might help. I always thought we were happy together, but there must have been something wrong to make him go. I can fix that."

"Him leaving had nothing to do with your marriage," I said. "Dad loved you. He must still love you."

"Not enough to stay with us." A rare frown tugged at her lips. "You should come home. This is too big for you to deal with on your own."

"I'm not on my own. I have Bandit with me. She's being... helpful."

"I'm indispensable," Bandit said. "Don't worry, Mrs. Crypt. I'm keeping an eye on Tempest. I'm making sure she's not getting in too much trouble."

"Tempest will figure this out," Aurora said, her voice quiet in the background. "And she's helping the angels with a murder investigation while she's there. She's very busy."

"That's true. And I really need to go figure out this murder." I was grateful for Aurora's intervention. I had to hope she didn't mention that Dad just happened to be a suspect in this investigation. "We've got people to interview."

Mom pursed her lips before nodding. "I don't like not knowing where you are. I'm worried about you."

"I'm fine. I'll catch up with you later." I said goodbye and ended the connection before my mom's sorrowful expression made me slip up and say something I may regret.

"Far be it for me to give you sensible advice, but if you don't reveal what's going on, this will blow up in your face." Bandit splayed her fingers and shot glitter everywhere.

"You don't think I know that?" I stood from the bed and grabbed my jacket. "There has to be a way to get Dad to remember who I am. Once he does, I bet the rest of his memories will fall into place. But I can't risk harming him if his memories were taken or suppressed. I need to know why it happened."

Bandit tapped me on the chest. "You still think it has to do with that demon hibernating inside you?"

"Very possibly. And if Frank is behind my dad's memory wipe, I bet there's a big scary reason behind it."

"You're not going to let your dad walk away, though?" Bandit asked. "I thought you wanted him back in your lives."

"More than anything." I headed to the door. "But I need to make sure he won't be harmed when we find out a way to reverse his mind wipe or whatever it was that happened to him. Let's get out of here. We have a fun lecture to attend."

"Do I really have to come?" Bandit dragged her feet as she followed me out of the motel.

"Of course. You're my backup. And you never know, you may learn something new."

Bandit grumbled all the way to the hall. There was a line of people entering as we arrived, most of them clutching books and talking in whispers as they waited to find a seat before the lecture started.

I bypassed the line and headed inside. I was hoping to get a jump on the crowd and see if I could talk to Jeremiah or any of the other suspects before we got trapped in the lecture hall.

"Ladies and gentlemen, please take your seats," an usher announced to the assembled crowd.

There was a rush as everyone hurried into the hall, racing to the front to get a good seat.

I lurked at the back with Bandit, trying to spot Herbert's party, but there were so many people hurrying in that it was hard to see through the mass of bodies and books.

"Maybe they're not going to show up," Bandit said. "We've come to this boring lecture for nothing."

"I doubt they'd miss this," I said. "And Saul and Jeremiah must be here since they're speaking.

We'll just have to listen to the talks and then grab Jeremiah at the end for a friendly chat about murder."

"If I haven't died of boredom first," Bandit said.

"If you wouldn't mind taking your seats now," an usher whispered to me, "the talks are about to start. We shut the doors once they begin to avoid people coming in late and causing a disturbance."

"This is our final chance to escape," Bandit said, looking longingly at the door.

"We're staying."

We snuck into two seats at the back and settled in. A couple of minutes later, the lights dimmed, and a spotlight illuminated a podium at the front.

A tall blonde guy with dark eyes appeared and walked to the podium. I recognized him from our encounter in the Angel Force office. That was Jeremiah.

"Welcome everyone to what I hope will be fascinating talks on the subject of demonology. My name is Jeremiah Tombe. I've been lecturing on the subject for over a decade. Some of you may be surprised to learn that I'm one quarter demon."

There was a murmur among the crowd, and people shifted in their seats.

He raised a hand, an indulgent smile on his face. "Don't worry. My good side prevails over the darkness. Most of the time."

A nervous chuckle came from the crowd.

Jeremiah had a warm, smooth voice. I was happy to listen to him discuss several case studies involving demons and the progress made in the study of demon control. He was intelligent and clearly enjoyed his subject.

Bandit fell asleep after the first five minutes. Her head rested on my shoulder as she softly snored. She jerked awake as the crowd applauded Jeremiah as he finished his talk.

"Is it over?" she asked.

"Jeremiah's talk is done."

"I hope you found the talk interesting," Jeremiah said.

"Not really," Bandit muttered.

"You were asleep for most of it. He was good. I learned a few things."

"I'm sleeping again if there's any more of this." She crossed her arms over her chest and tipped her head back.

"Please welcome Saul Connelly to the stage. He is a dear friend and colleague of mine," Jeremiah said. He waited a moment as the audience applauded. "Saul has a lifelong interest in demonology and worked closely with the late Herbert Winkler to forge a path toward a cure for demonism. He has fascinating insights about the long-term future of demons and how we may be able to control them." He stepped back and extended a hand.

The crowd applauded again as Saul appeared.

He took his place at the podium before looking around the crowd. "Thank you for the warm welcome. I'm not accustomed to public speaking, so I'll keep this short. We had a great loss recently in our community. I'm sure many of you were devastated by the news of Professor Winkler's death. We're all mourning his loss. He was a close friend of mine for many years. I still can't believe that I'll never hear him talk again." Saul's head lowered for a second.

The crowd murmured gently, and lots of people shook their heads.

"But fear not. Professor Winkler's work will go on," Saul said. "As you have just heard, we have the very best experts on our team working to develop the final version of the cure for demonism. Along with my colleagues, I plan to take the helm of Professor Winkler's empire and lead it to a promising future. A future that will mean a safer world for all magic users and non-magic users alike."

"He doesn't know what he's talking about," Bandit muttered. "There's no cure for demonism. You have to have demons or you don't have angels. There has to be a natural balance. What would the angels do if there were no demons to bother them?"

"Take long lunches and polish their halos?"

She snorted a laugh. "This whole concept is a joke. This lot are just conning money out of idiots from book sales and this tour."

A man in the row in front of us turned and shushed Bandit.

She shrugged. "It's true."

I nodded. "Saul confirmed that Herbert would have become a wealthy man, thanks to this book and the demon cure. Where there's money to be made, there'll always be people lurking around trying to take it."

"Including the people Herbert surrounded himself with. The smug guy on stage not excluded." Bandit inclined her head toward the podium.

Saul spoke for another twenty minutes about the tour plans, book launch, and training events before wrapping things up.

I hopped from my seat and nudged Bandit. "Let's see if we can get backstage. I want to have a proper talk with Jeremiah. If he's now the brains of this operation, he also has a vested interest in getting rid of the competition."

We pushed through the crowd and headed behind the stage.

"I told you to sort out the lights." Saul stood in front of Brendan, glaring down at him.

"I did exactly as you asked." Brendan took a step back, blinking up at Saul. "The stagehand said it would be sorted."

"You clearly didn't give him the right instructions. I was sweating under those lights. That doesn't look professional. My reputation must remain impeccable."

"I'm sorry. It won't happen again."

"If it does, you're fired. Herbert may have put up with your incompetence, but I won't. Now I'm in charge, you'll have to make more of an effort. You need to sort yourself out." Saul barged past Brendan and stomped along the corridor.

Brendan watched him go, his shoulders sagging.

"Hey, is everything okay?" I strode over with Bandit.

Brendan whirled around and stared up at me. He licked his lips. "Oh, that was nothing. I just made a mistake. He was right to tell me so."

More like Saul was a bully who picked on people to make himself feel like a big man. "It's Brendan, isn't it?"

He nodded. "That's right."

"Have you got a minute to talk? I'm working with the angels to figure out what happened to Herbert."

His eyes widened. "Um, I guess so. I need to tidy up before I can leave. Saul likes everything kept neat."

"I'll be quick. How long did you work with Herbert?"

"Just over two years. He took me on as his apprentice when I started at university."

"How did he treat you? I'm guessing better than Saul."

Brendan rubbed the back of his neck. "Saul's not so bad. But he has to have everything just so. I admired Professor Winkler. And you're right; he treated me well."

"What's going to happen to your apprenticeship now Herbert's gone?" I asked.

"I'm not sure. Everything feels up in the air," he said. "I had another year to apprentice under Professor Winkler. I'm training to be a demonologist."

"You're very small to be a demonologist," Bandit said. "Most demons will eat you in a few bites. Yum, yum."

Brendan swallowed as he stared at Bandit's sharp teeth. "It's what I have to do. My family was killed by demons. It's important that demons don't gain the upper hand in the battle between light and darkness. If the cure can be given to all demons, just think what a difference that will make. A world without demons."

I touched my chest. I wouldn't mind simply having the one inside me removed. "Where were you when you learned about Herbert?"

"I was here in the back room, working on some lab reports and checking through tour schedules to make sure we'd have space to work. Some of these venues can be cramped."

"Were you alone?"

"No, Saul was there most of the time. He always double-checks my work." Brendan ducked his head. "I stepped out for twenty minutes to get some dinner."

"Can anyone confirm that?"

His eyes widened. "I'm sure they can. The lady in the Orange Pumpkin Cafe will remember me. I, um, well, I had an accident and spilled my soup. And I bumped into Molvos' associate on my way."

"You mean Abel Cross?" I asked.

"That's right. He was leaving a bar. He looked in a terrible mood and shoved me out of the way."

"What impression do you have of Abel?"

"He's a scary guy. Virginia keeps saying he was involved in what happened to Professor Winkler."

"Is that what you think?" I asked.

"Everyone says it was Molvos," Brendan said, "and it makes sense. Professor Winkler pushed his test subjects hard. I worried that some weren't mentally strong enough to endure the treatments."

"I heard that Molvos didn't willingly enter the trials for this cure."

"Not many of the demons we test on do," he said. "That didn't bother Professor Winkler. He didn't create the cure so demons could voluntarily administer it to themselves."

"What are you suggesting?" I said. "Herbert planned to give the cure to other magic users?"

"Exactly right." Brendan smiled. "It was such a clever idea. It was to be a weapon against the demons. A way of keeping them in their place. If they know they could lose their powers if they attack someone, they'll think twice about it."

"I bet the demons weren't happy about that," I said.

"They hated it. Professor Winkler got a lot of death threats because of his work," Brendan said. "But he was determined not to give up. Neither are we. We're carrying on his work. If only my family had had this protection when they were attacked, I wouldn't be an orphan." His head dipped. "And now, I've lost Professor Winkler as well. I won't stop until this cure is out there for everyone to use."

I patted him on the shoulder. Here was a man on a mission. "Thanks for talking to us."

"I'd better get on. I've got work to do." Brendan scurried away.

"There's a guy who lives on his nerves," Bandit said.

"And a guy who lives with vengeance in his heart every day." I nodded. "Do you fancy a snack?"

"Always."

"Good. Let's go check out Brendan's alibi."

Chapter 12

We entered the Orange Pumpkin Cafe, and I spent a couple of minutes perusing the delicious treats behind the glass case as we waited in line to speak to the server.

"What can I get you?" a round-faced woman with a bright smile said. "We've got Cherry Bakewell as the special today if you're looking for something sweet."

"Actually, we're not here for—"

"Yes. We'll have that whole Cherry Bakewell, half a dozen chocolate chip brownies, six pecan caramel cookies, and some of that strawberry tart." Bandit glanced at me. "What are you going to have?"

I shook my head. "I'll take a coffee to go."

"Right you are." The woman began piling up Bandit's order.

"I wonder if you could help me with something," I said. "Do you remember a guy with ginger hair and red eyes who came in here and ordered soup two nights ago?"

She glanced up and smiled. "That poor guy is hard to forget. He spilled his food all down his shirt. He'd ordered minestrone soup to take out, along with a bag of cheese and bacon rolls and a sweet flan. He was trying to balance it all when someone walked into him. The soup tipped down his front. I felt so sorry for him. He couldn't have been more apologetic, though. I gave him another soup on the house, but I think his shirt was ruined."

That ruled Brendan out of the equation in this investigation. He'd been with Saul, then in here to get food during the time of Herbert's murder. I didn't have him as a key suspect, anyway. He seemed too nervy to go up against a demon.

I grudgingly paid for Bandit's enormous food order and was turning to leave the cafe when Jeremiah. Virginia, and several other people I didn't recognize walked in.

"You get eating," I said to Bandit as I passed her the bag of food. "That's just the man I want to see."

I hurried to the table Jeremiah was settling at. "Hello again, Virginia."

She looked up and half-smiled. "Hi, Tempest. How are things going with the investigation?"

"We're getting there," I said. "I wouldn't mind talking to you, Jeremiah. I was hoping to see you at the lecture."

He glanced at Virginia, and she nodded. "Of course. I've heard that you spoke to Virginia about what happened to Herbert. Would you like to join us?"

I shook my head. "This will only take a couple of minutes. Tell me how you knew Herbert,"

"He started out as my mentor. I went to university later in life and was fortunate enough to have him as a tutor. We became friends. When he started touring to promote his work, he asked me to join him. It was a privilege to work alongside him. It's such a shame he's gone."

Virginia patted his hand. "We all feel his absence."

Jeremiah smiled at her. "I always knew he was vulnerable because of his work."

"The death threats, you mean?" I said.

"Demons hated his hunt for a cure," Jeremiah said. "I was so worried for my friend. He even had his apartment broken into on several occasions."

"Was that reported to the angels?" I asked.

"Yes, he always told them what was going on. And he kept records of the threats he received. The angels have all the information if you need to look at it."

Housebreaking didn't seem like a demon sort of thing to do. If a demon wanted to get you, they ripped the door off its hinges, or burned a hole in the wall, and grabbed you. Breaking into someone's home seemed far too civilized.

"I'll be glad when the angels formally charge Molvos and Abel," Jeremiah said. "You must almost be finished with the investigation by now."

"Everyone in your party is so convinced it was those two," I said. "It's almost as if you've gotten together to make sure you all have your stories straight. You wouldn't do that, would you?"

He sat up straight in his seat. "Of course not. Why would we need to have our stories straight? None of us killed Herbert. And if you knew Abel Cole like I do, you'd have no doubt he has to be involved. That man is dark through and through. I wouldn't be surprised if he doesn't have demon blood flowing through him."

I grimaced. "Much like you."

"We're nothing alike. My demon energy is weak. I make a point of keeping it under control. I find good routines, lots of meditation, and some of the drugs Herbert was trialing effective. I barely have any dark thoughts."

"You really think Abel has turned to the dark side?" I said. "He would murder in cold blood?" I should stick to confirming what Jeremiah had been doing when Herbert was killed, but every time I heard my dad's name, I lost focus.

"I've no doubt of it. He's destroyed people's lives. He takes happiness and sucks it away like he considers it a poison."

"It sounds like he's done something to you personally."

"Not to me but my brother. He got into some problems with debt. Abel was paid to remind him that he needed to return what was owed. My brother ended up in the hospital for three weeks. He hasn't been the same since."

I resisted the urge to shake Jeremiah and tell him he was lying. My dad would never do such a thing. I repressed a sigh. Maybe he wouldn't have ten years ago, but anything was possible now.

"Where were you when you learned of Herbert's death?"

He glanced at Virginia again. "On my own in the library. I was tweaking my talk for the tour presentation."

"Can anyone vouch for your whereabouts?"

His mouth twisted to the side. "Sadly not. Herbert made an arrangement for us to use the library out of hours because we needed a quiet place to work. They were happy to assist us and even gave us our own key to come and go as we pleased."

Bandit strolled over and offered me a half-eaten brownie.

I shook my head and pushed it away. "How did you find out about Herbert?"

"Virginia told me. We raced back to the house as quickly as we could."

"Did you see Molvos or Abel around the house when you arrived?"

"No, although Saul saw Molvos. I trust his word. It has to be that demon. It was either him or his dark companion. Abel Cross is as much a demon as Molvos. Anyone would think he had a demon inside him."

"That's where you're wrong. His daughter hosts the demon," Bandit said.

I nudged her with an elbow and glared at her.

"Oh! You mean Zandra?" Jeremiah said.

I stared at him. "Who's Zandra?"

"That's Abel's daughter."

Chapter 13

I grabbed Bandit's arm, shock making my knees shake. "Abel has a daughter?"

"Yes. I've never met her, but I've heard mention of her. I figured that was who you were talking about." Jeremiah's expression grew concerned. "Are you okay? You don't look too good."

Bandit curled a wing around me. "If you'll excuse us, we have food to eat." She turned and hustled me out of the cafe while I could still stand.

My legs moved on autopilot as my head spun. A daughter? Dad had another daughter?

"Let's get out of here before you fall over." Bandit shot into the air and zoomed over the trees before dropping down outside the motel a few minutes later.

I couldn't breathe properly. My brain felt fried. I staggered into the room and stood there, staring at the wall. What did this mean?

"Here, eat this." Bandit shoved a cookie in my mouth.

I bit down, not tasting the gooey sweetness. "Did I just hear that right?"

Bandit set the food down before turning to me. "You did. Abel has another kid."

"I have a half-sister," I said.

"Yep. Eat more cookie." Bandit shoved the rest of the cookie in my mouth. "You're in shock. The sugar will help."

I chewed and swallowed, not tasting anything.

She tilted her head as her gaze ran over me. "You need something more hard-core than sugar." Her wings swooped over me several times, and I was soon covered in warm sparkly glitter.

Every nerve in my body calmed, and I sank onto the bed. "What did you just do to me?"

"I'm glittering you until you come to your senses," she said.

I blinked and scrubbed glitter out of my eyes. "But... how did this happen?"

Bandit sat next to me and wrapped a wing around my shoulders. "You should have had this conversation with your parents a long time ago. There's a thing that happens when a mommy and daddy love one another-"

"Not funny," I growled out. "You know what this means. Dad cheated on Mom."

Bandit's wings fluttered out around her. "I understand how sucky this situation is, but you must remember, he doesn't know who you are. As far as Abel's concerned, he was never married. He never had a family. He doesn't remember any of you."

My eyes stung with tears, and I blinked them away. "How can I keep this a secret?"

"Will it help your mom to know what your dad's been up to behind her back?"

"She'll be devastated. They were such a sweet couple. I used to pretend to be annoyed at how perfect they were, but they were the poster couple of relationship goals. They had a happy marriage."

"I bet they'd still be happy if your dad could remember you," Bandit said. "You can't say anything about this. Not yet."

"Not so long ago, you were telling me not to keep secrets from my family."

"Jeremiah may have gotten things wrong. What if Zandra isn't Abel's daughter? She could be a friend's kid or an orphan he's taken pity on. Drop this bombshell without all the facts, and there'll be trouble."

I groaned. "I suppose this is just another secret to add to the ever-growing pile that will crush me if I'm not careful. I need to find Zandra," I said.

"How's that going to help?"

"I need the facts. And she's my sister. I mean, I have to know all about her." I rubbed my hand across my face. "Maybe she can tell me what happened to my dad. Our dad. Where he's been all this time. I don't even know how old she is. What if she's closer to my age? That would mean..." My words vanished. Had Dad really cheated on Mom?

"You're freaking out about nothing. From what Jeremiah said, it sounds like she's not around much. Maybe they aren't close."

"That doesn't matter. Her very existence means—"

"Don't we have a murder to solve? One that your dad is implicated in?"

I groaned and slumped back on the bed. "What do I do? I want to meet Zandra, but I also have to keep Dad out of jail."

More glitter rained down on me, and my anxiety ebbed to a manageable roar as it lurked in the back of my mind.

"Do you want my advice on this potentially life-changing matter?"

"You're my sounding board," I said. "Hit me with something useful."

"If I was in this terrible position, first off, I'd eat some delicious treats." Bandit folded her wings behind her. "And since you've had a shock, I'm happy to share two more of my special treats with you."

"The treats I bought you?"

"We're not keeping count of such small things."

"Thanks. But I don't feel like—" A brownie was stuffed into my mouth.

"Second, I'd focus on the murder. It's no good getting your dad back if he gets charged with murder and put behind bars for the rest of his life. That will only add to your family's problems. Aurora definitely won't be happy if you mess up this case because of some long-lost sister you didn't know you had until five minutes ago. A half-sister at that. A sister who may not even be real."

I chewed on the brownie. Bandit was making a lot of sense. Dad was still in the frame for Herbert's murder, and everyone was pointing the finger at him and Molvos. I had to prove their innocence before I did anything else. As much as I wanted to focus on fixing my family and meeting my new sister, I had to clear his name first.

"Are you thinking clearly yet?" Bandit asked. "I have plenty more glitter if you need it."

"Yeah, I'm good. Thanks for the nudge."

"It's what I'm here for," Bandit said. "So, who's left on the suspect list? We can discount Brendan. He alibis out."

"And we can discount my dad," I said.

"Are you sure about that?" Bandit asked. "Brendan did bump into him leaving the bar around the time Herbert was killed."

"Yes, I'm sure. And he even told us he left the bar on the night of the murder. He didn't hide that piece of information."

"Maybe he left to go commit murder. He simply left that bit out when you spoke."

"Not helping," I muttered.

"I'm simply playing fairies advocate," she said.

"My dad isn't the killer. And it can't be Molvos. They alibi for each other."

"If either of them can be trusted," Bandit said.

I glared at her. "Let's assume they can. Next suspect."

"Okay, I understand you have a certain bias toward your dad being innocent. I'm going to tuck him at the very bottom of the suspect list."

"You do what you have to do," I said. "Who does that leave us with?"

"We have the slightly smarmy Saul."

"Who'll make a ton of money now Herbert's out of the picture," I said. "But he was with Brendan."

"He had a small window of opportunity when Brendan went to get food," Bandit said. "And Saul was close to the house. Remember, Molvos ran into him. Would it have been hard for him to kill Herbert and then double back with the intention of looking like the innocent party who discovered his friend mauled to death by a demon?"

"It's possible that happened." I pressed my fingers against the bridge of my nose. I was having a hard time focusing.

"We also have the former girlfriend who may have jealousy issues," Bandit said.

"And she has no alibi," I said. "She may spend her nights alone with her nose in a book, but that could be a cover. She could have snuck out and committed murder."

"A very definite possibility. Although Virginia seems sweet. She's more research nerd than ruthless ninja."

"Maybe she's hiding a dark secret," I said. "Sometimes, nerds snap."

"Much like you." Bandit chuckled as she stuffed a cookie in my mouth before I could protest. "Finally, we come to the best friend."

"Another one without an alibi that can be confirmed," I said around my mouthful of cookie. "And someone who's gunning for my dad. Jeremiah's convinced Dad was involved in this murder."

"He could be deflecting," Bandit said. "Jeremiah's pointing the finger at your dad and Molvos because they're such obvious suspects. You get enough people telling a lie and it can become the truth."

"Is this revenge for what my dad did to his brother?" I asked. "Or does he want top spot on the tour circuit and a share of some of that money?"

"I don't think it's either of those things," Bandit said. "Did you notice how comforting Virginia was being when they were in the cafe? And the way Jeremiah looked at Virginia before answering your questions?"

I sat up and stared at Bandit. "You think they're in a relationship?"

"Virginia was sitting very close to him."

"I figured she was just being comforting," I said. "They are friends."

"Maybe they've been comforting each other without any clothes on from time to time. It was obvious to me," Bandit said. "She even squeezed his knee when she thought no one was looking. I was standing by the door, so I saw everything."

"I guess I was still reeling over the revelation that I have a half-sister and missed that going down." That was my mistake. I normally picked up on that kind of thing.

Bandit shrugged. "It could be worse. You could have a half-brother."

My gut tightened. "Could there be more than one sibling out there? Maybe there are half a dozen children my dad's fathered since he's been away."

Bandit tapped me on the forehead. "You're getting off the important subject again. We're hunting for a killer and need to clear your dad's name. If we don't, he'll be a worthless father to have, no matter how many children he's had since he ran away from you."

"He didn't run away."

"So say you."

"I know he didn't leave willingly."

Bandit raised a hand. "I believe you. Okay, back to murder. This could be a case of the jealous ex-girlfriend and the slighted best friend getting together and deciding to do away with Herbert. Maybe he didn't approve of their relationship, or they got worried he might try to ruin them if it got out they were seeing each other. A lot of people loved Herbert for his work."

I swung my legs as I sat on the edge of the bed. All I could focus on was finding Zandra and speaking to her. Bandit was right. Dad had been away for years. He could have been busy in that time and had dozens of children with lots of different women.

Bandit jabbed me with the tip of her wing. "Shall we speak to Virginia and Jeremiah again? Ask them how serious their relationship is?"

I nodded. "I should go see my dad first."

"And ask about all the half-siblings you have? That won't confuse him for a second. He doesn't even know you're his daughter." Bandit grabbed a brownie and ate it, her gaze not leaving mine.

"What? Why are you staring at me?"

She finished her brownie and reached for another. "You're worse than useless. You need to focus."

"I'm trying. I've had a shock."

"Is this something you can get past?"

I let out a sigh. "No! I don't know. Eventually."

"Then it's time to take a rest."

"I can't rest. Everything's a mess. Everything—"
As Bandit's glitter rained down on me, my eyes
closed, and the room went black.

Chapter 14

I blinked, and my gaze went around the room. I was on my bed in the motel; the curtains were drawn, and there was a faint smell of cake in the air.

I rolled over and came face-to-face with a sleeping Bandit. I poked her shoulder with a finger. "What did you do to me?"

Her eyes opened, and she grinned. "Good morning to you."

I growled in her face. "Tell me what you did."

"Yuck. Morning breath alert. I helped you. You were spiraling. I needed you to relax before you popped a blood vessel."

I scratched my fingers through my hair. They came away covered in glitter. "You fairy glittered me into unconsciousness?"

"It's the best way to go. My glitter can calm you, excite you, and knock you out. It's a one size fits all sort of ability. You needed to relax. I get that you had a shock, but you weren't concentrating on the murder."

As much as I wanted to be angry, it felt like I'd had the most amazing sleep. I rolled off the bed and stood. "I'm focused now."

"So am I. Let's get a huge breakfast."

"We can eat after we've seen Virginia and Jeremiah. We lost time thanks to your glitter games."

"You mean, thanks to my amazing powers and ability to control a panicking witch who was about to make a huge mistake and ruin everything."

There was a small tap on the motel door. Bandit hopped up and opened it.

A tiny angel fluttered in on an air current and cleared her throat. "Angels' greetings to you both. You have been invited to breakfast at Sophie's apartment."

I wrinkled my nose. "We were just about to go to the cafe."

"No! Let's go to the angel's place. Her breakfasts are amazing," Bandit said.

"Shall I tell her you'll be coming?" the tiny angel asked.

"Yep. We'll be there in ten minutes," Bandit said. "Two if I fly us over."

"We'll walk," I said.

"A sweet day to you both." The angel nodded before fluttering out of the room.

I shoved my feet into my boots, combed glitter out of my hair, and headed out of the motel room with Bandit.

Sophie was standing by the elevator door when we arrived at her penthouse apartment. "I'm so glad you could make it." She ushered us into the kitchen. "You look sparkly today, Tempest."

"Blame Bandit," I said.

Sophie smiled. "It suits you. I thought it would be appropriate to catch up about the Herbert Winkler incident, providing it doesn't put you off of eating."

"Nothing stops me from eating," Bandit said. She nudged me. "Told you this would be another epic breakfast feast."

I licked my lips as I admired the table laden with breakfast treats, the smell of warm fresh bread in the air and freshly brewed coffee perking me right up.

"Delightful," Sophie said. "I hope I have your favorites."

"You do. There's nothing like a bit of murder and muffins first thing in the morning," Bandit said.

"Oh! I didn't make muffins. I could run out and get some." Sophie's wings fluttered as she looked at the food-laden table.

"There's no need for muffins. There's enough to feed an army here. This is perfect." I settled in my seat and grabbed a croissant.

Sophie settled in her seat. "So, how's it all going?"

"We're interested in the relationship between Virginia and Jeremiah," I said.

"Relationship?" Sophie poured coffee for us.

"When you spoke with them, were they open about being together?" I asked.

Sophie tilted her head as she spooned fruit salad into her bowl. "No, I didn't realize they were together. Do you think that's important to what happened to Herbert?"

"It could be," I said.

"We reckon they killed Herbert," Bandit said. "Maybe he didn't like them being together. He didn't approve of their relationship, tried to put a stop to it, so they did him in."

"Goodness! What a thought," Sophie said.

"Can you have them brought to the station so I can question them?" I asked.

"Of course. There's paperwork to complete before that can happen, though. Two form B12s and a yellow form D1. Give me a moment. I'll contact one of my angels and get the paperwork underway. We can't bring people into the office without the right forms signed."

I grinned at Bandit. "Of course not."

Sophie left us alone for fifteen minutes while she spoke to an angel over her snow globe in the lounge. During that time, I ate three croissants, while Bandit consumed five pain aux chocolate, three giant waffles, and a platter of fruit.

"The paperwork is underway." Sophie returned to the table. "Would you like more croissants?"

"Yes, please," Bandit said.

"No, thanks," I said. "We've had plenty."

"I've asked Virginia and Jeremiah to come to the station as soon as possible. Hopefully, by the time we get there, they should be waiting. We can clear up this matter. I'm surprised you think they're involved."

"I've ruled out Brendan as a suspect," I said. "He has a good alibi. And it seems unlikely it was Saul, although there was a small window of opportunity. He'd have needed to time it perfectly to avoid being discovered at the crime scene."

"What about Molvos? We still have him in custody," Sophie said. "And then there's Abel."

"I don't think either of them is involved," I said. "They alibi for each other."

"I'm not comfortable excluding them from this investigation," Sophie said. "But, of course, you're the expert when it comes to these unfortunate incidents."

"We aren't ruling them out," Bandit said. "Tempest is just biased."

"About a bounty hunter and his demon sidekick?" Sophie's brow wrinkled.

"I'm not biased," I said. "I keep an open mind. Just because somebody has a dark past, it doesn't automatically make them a bad person."

"Of course. We like to give people a fair chance," Sophie said. "But how many chances should an individual get?"

"Let's see what the interviews with Virginia and Jeremiah turn up before we grill Abel and Molvos again." I nudged Bandit. "Right?"

"Whatever you say. After all, you're the expert." She hooked a piece of pineapple and ate it.

"Excellent. Do excuse me for a few minutes. I must get ready before we leave for the office." Sophie left the table to do goodness knows what since she already looked immaculate, while I slummed it in the clothes I wore yesterday.

I glared at Bandit. "We don't need the angels finding out that Abel is my dad. They might stop me from investigating."

"You have to admit you're looking at him through rose-tinted glasses. He could be involved."

"And he could be innocent," I said. "I prefer that option."

"Which is where the bias comes in," Bandit said.

"Eat your fruit and stop causing trouble."

Bandit chuckled and threw a grape in the air before catching it with her teeth.

Ten minutes later, we were out the door of Sophie's apartment and hurrying through the chilly morning air.

"The weather is still weird," Bandit said. "I thought this place was supposed to have a constant temperature."

"It should be a pleasant twenty-one degrees all year round," Sophie said. "We think it's a slight imbalance in the magical order that's causing the disharmony. Because of the unfortunate incident, everyone is unsettled. It makes it harder to keep large spells, such as the weather spell blanketing Puzzlewood, constant. Of course, once this matter is resolved, everything will go back to normal. I'm confident of that." She nodded a greeting at the angel at the reception desk when we arrived. "Have Virginia Lupin and Jeremiah Tombe arrived for their interviews?"

"They have. I put them in interview rooms one and two," the angel said.

"Perfect." Sophie smiled at me. "Who do you want to start with?"

"Let's begin with Virginia," I said.

"You go through and begin the interview," Sophie said. "I need to double-check the paperwork and make sure it's filed."

I walked through the office with Bandit once we'd signed our authorization forms, located interview room one, and headed in.

Virginia sat at a small table, her hands clasped in front of her and a nervous expression on her face.

I settled at the table as Bandit paced around the room.

"Is there something I can help you with?" Virginia asked. "I was surprised when the angels requested my presence."

"You can. I'm interested in your relationship with Jeremiah," I said.

Her shoulders inched up. "What relationship?"

"Are you dating?"

Virginia glanced down at her hands. "We've worked together for a while. He's a nice man."

"Which doesn't answer my question," I said. "Are you in a romantic relationship with Jeremiah?"

"I... respect him. We work together. That's all."

"You're not hiding your relationship for any reason?" I asked. "Herbert didn't find out and warn you off Jeremiah?"

"No! Nothing like that. Herbert and I were separated for a long time before he died. I was still fond of the man, but I wasn't in love with him. We were free to date other people."

"And did you date other people?"

"One or two."

"No one stuck?"

She shifted in her seat. "I was busy with work."

"And how did you feel about Herbert putting his work before you?" I said. "You must have been angry that the relationship failed because of his obsession."

"That wasn't the reason it failed." She sighed. "At least, that wasn't the only reason. We weren't right for each other. I was star-struck when I met him. Herbert was the top of his field in demonology. He was smart, knowledgeable, and ambitious when it came to finding the cure. I was flattered when he became interested in me and asked me out. I let it go to my head. I soon realized we weren't right together."

"And Herbert didn't like that?"

"He understood. And you were right; his work was his passion. So long as he had that, I knew he'd never be lonely. I was grateful when he gave me this job. He could have tossed me to one side. He was a good man."

"There were no problems between you?"

"None. I considered him a friend. Why do you want to know all this? I've already explained my relationship status with Herbert."

"Just to be clear, you weren't dating Jeremiah to get back at Herbert?"

"Oh! Absolutely not."

"Herbert didn't find it hard to accept that his best friend was dating you?"

"No, because we aren't dating." Virginia lifted her chin and glared at me.

I couldn't decide if that expression was defiance or stubbornness. "Wait here." I stood from my seat. "I'll be back in a few minutes. Bandit, keep an eye on things."

"Sure thing," she said, flashing a smile at Virginia.

I left the room and headed to interview room two.

Jeremiah stood by the wall. He straightened when he saw me. "Hi, Tempest. Is everything okay?"

"I've just had an interesting conversation with Virginia," I said.

"I met her in the reception area when I arrived. What do the angels want with us? They said it was urgent. Does this have something to do with Herbert?"

"The angels and I want to know about your relationship with Virginia," I said. "You're more than just work colleagues."

His hand went to his pocket before he withdrew it. "What makes you say that?"

"The way you behaved around each other in the cafe yesterday," I said. "How long has it been going on?"

"Why is that relevant to this murder investigation?"

"You don't deny that you're seeing each other?"

He was silent for several seconds. "Before I answer that, tell me how it's relevant to what happened to Herbert."

"I think Herbert disapproved of your relationship. He warned you off Virginia. Maybe he told you to keep away from her. You didn't want to do that. You could have argued. Things got out of hand."

Jeremiah shook his head. "That never happened. I had a deep respect for Herbert. I'd never do anything to make him unhappy."

"Even if it meant missing out on a chance at happiness with Virginia?"

"I see where you're going with this." He slumped against the wall. "I'm surprised the angels haven't picked up on it sooner. I have been seeing Virginia. I'm crazy about her."

"And you needed to get your rival out of the way?"

"No! You've got this all wrong. Herbert wasn't a rival for Virginia's affections. He was more like a father figure to both of us. It felt a bit like I was asking for Virginia's hand in marriage when I approached Herbert and told him I'd developed feelings for her and wanted to ask her on a date."

"And he didn't like it?"

"He was fine about it. Herbert wanted us to be happy. And we are. Ridiculously happy." He pushed his hand back into his pocket and drew out a small black box. "So happy that I plan to propose to her. I got the ring the first day we arrived in Puzzlewood. I'm waiting for the right moment to ask."

"Why keep your relationship a secret if everyone was happy about it?"

"We thought it was for the best. People jump to assumptions and think the worst, much like you are. She'll make me so happy." A soppy smile crossed his face. "Of course, I need to get Virginia to say yes to my proposal."

"Remind me again of your alibi on the night of Herbert's murder," I said. "Were you really alone at the library?"

Jeremiah shook his head. "No, I was with Virginia. We thought it would be easier to say we were alone doing separate research in the library."

"Lying about your alibi is suspicious," I said. "It suggests you're hiding something."

His shoulders drooped. "I know that now. I discussed what to do with Virginia. She said we had to keep things simple. We didn't want tongues wagging. She's worried about her reputation, first dating Herbert and then me. And having a relationship with someone you work with can be difficult. I agreed with her. I'd do anything for that woman."

"Wait right here," I said. "I need to talk to Virginia again." I left the room and shut the door behind me. I walked back into interview room one.

"You see, my wings almost touch either side of the walls." Bandit stood in front of a terrified looking Virginia, her wings extended.

I gestured for her to stop before sitting opposite Virginia. "So, good news. Jeremiah has told me everything."

She blinked several times. "What has he told you?"

"He's in the clear for Herbert's murder," I said.

Her mouth fell open. "What do you mean by that? Is he blaming me for what happened to Herbert?"

"Should he be blaming you?" I arched an eyebrow.

Her mouth flapped open and shut several times. "No! I have nothing to hide. I'm not a killer. Jeremiah would never say I was."

"Maybe not. But you lied about your alibi on the night of Herbert's murder."

"Oooh! This is getting good." Bandit rubbed her hands together. "Jeremiah is a snitch. He told all to save his own skin."

Virginia swallowed, before letting out a sigh. "Jeremiah told you we were together when Herbert was killed?"

"Correct. And he told me that you asked him to keep quiet about your relationship. Why would that be?" I asked.

She gestured to me and frowned. "Because of this. I knew we'd face scrutiny, and people would think the worst of our romantic entanglement. They'd think I'd gotten together with Jeremiah and we cooked up some devious plan to get rid of Herbert. They'd assume that, because I was with Herbert before Jeremiah, there must have been a problem between us. Or maybe I cheated on him with Jeremiah and he found out."

"And is that—"

"Not true." Virginia tapped her hands on the table. "I cared for Herbert, but he was wrong for me. And as I got to know Jeremiah, I fell in love with him."

"That's sickeningly sweet," Bandit said. "Would you kill for the love of your life?"

"I didn't kill Herbert," Virginia said. "I was with Jeremiah that evening in the library."

"And Herbert knew about your relationship with Jeremiah?" I asked.

"He did. He didn't mind. He was so focused on fine tuning his work in the lead up to his new book release that he barely noticed the two of us."

The interview room door burst open, and Jeremiah stumbled in.

"Jeremiah!" Virginia jumped to her feet.

"I'm so sorry. I told Tempest everything," he said. "I hate hiding our relationship. It doesn't feel right. I want to shout from the rooftops how much I love you. Virginia, I want to spend the rest of my life with you."

"Maybe now isn't the right time to get all emotional," I said. I had a horrible feeling where this was going. "We're in the middle of an interview about your friend's murder."

Jeremiah continued as if he hadn't heard me. "Virginia, I adore you. I've never loved anyone as much as I love you."

Virginia glanced at me and giggled. "That's sweet of you."

He dropped to one knee and produced the black box from his pocket. He flipped it open to reveal a sparkling diamond. "I want to spend the rest of my life with you. Will you marry me?"

I groaned and rolled my eyes. That was the least romantic proposal in the world, ever.

Virginia's hand went to her chest as if she was having palpitations, and her eyes filled with tears. "You want to marry me?"

"This is so cute," Bandit said. She nudged Virginia with her wing. "What are you going to say?"

"Yes! A thousand times yes. Of course, I'll marry you." She flung her arms around Jeremiah's neck, and they kissed before laughing as he placed the ring on her finger.

Bandit tossed glitter over their heads and danced around them. "Congratulations! And just to be clear, neither of you murdered Herbert?"

Jeremiah stood and clasped Virginia to his side. "I can assure you we were together when Herbert was killed."

I tipped my head back. It looked like they were in the clear. Unless they were doing a great job of covering for each other, the only thing I'd discovered were two love-struck fools who had no opportunity to murder Herbert.

"Thanks for your time," I said. "You're free to go. Congrats on the engagement."

Jeremiah led Virginia out of the room, their hands clasped together.

"Young love. Isn't it great?" Bandit wrapped a wing around my shoulder and squeezed me.

"It's not great for us. They didn't kill Herbert. What do we do now?"

"I'm thinking we speak to Molvos and Abel again. Their alibis aren't airtight, and they are known for being naughty."

I hated the idea of interrogating my dad again. I wanted one of the other suspects to hold their hands up and confess so I could get on with jogging my dad's memory and then we could go home. "Okay, let's go hunt out Abel."

"I think that's an excellent idea, but we need a break first," Bandit said. "After all, we have just scrubbed two suspects off the list. That is cause to celebrate."

"What do you have in mind?"

She grinned. "Come with me. I've got the perfect thing to relieve your stress."

Chapter 15

I scowled at Bandit as we stood in front of the Puzzlewood magical maze. "I'm not going in."

"If you discount the water park, this is the best thing about Puzzlewood. Inside the maze there are treasures, treats, and even a grand prize at the center. Nobody knows what the grand prize is because no one has ever made it to the center. It could be anything."

"This won't relieve my stress," I said. "Getting lost in an enormous maze will make it worse."

"Fresh air and exercise always helps. And you won't know until you try," Bandit said. "This will take your mind off the problem. If you aren't obsessing over your dad's innocence, you could find a solution. Inspiration will strike, and you'll figure out who really killed Herbert."

"A sit down with a large mug of tea and a big sticky bun may also have the same effect."

"We can do that after we've conquered this maze." Bandit grabbed my hand and yanked me to the entrance. "Give up fighting me. I'm bigger than you and five times as strong. Don't make me bring out my angry glitter."

There was nothing I could do but allow the mildly terrifying fairy to drag me to the entrance to the maze.

I missed Wiggles as my sidekick. He'd always pick sticky buns over magical mazes. Dealing with this giant, egotistical fairy was another level of complicated.

"Isn't it amazing?" Bandit laughed. "An amazing maze. We're going to have so much fun. And I always think better when I'm having fun. I could even come up with the solution to this murder. A few hours strolling around this maze, hunting down treasures and looking for the grand prize, and it could all be wrapped up."

"We're not staying a few hours. Half an hour and that's it."

"You'll change your mind once we get going," Bandit said.

I skulked along behind her, seething as she bounced around, chattering excitedly about how she would get the grand prize.

"I reckon it could be a new house. Or maybe a pot of gold. It could be a lifetime supply of cream puff doughnuts. There are so many options." She thumped me with a wing. "What if you get to choose the grand prize? I need to do some serious thinking. I must ensure I make the right choice."

"Why don't you seriously think about Herbert's murder? Isn't that what this is all about?"

She glared at me as we walked into the maze. "You are no fun."

"I can be lots of fun. But I've got a lot on my mind."

"Sure you have. A missing father found with no memory, a half-sister discovered, a murder to solve and no clue who did it. It could be worse."

"How could it be worse?" I turned a corner and was met with a wall of greenery.

"You could have Wiggles with you, breaking wind and stealing your food."

I wanted that so badly. I wanted to go home. Part of me wished I'd never come to Puzzlewood. What if I blew the family apart with this discovery? What if Dad never got his memory back? Or if he did remember us but didn't want us anymore? Life moved on. Maybe he'd moved on too much and wouldn't want to go back.

I flinched as Bandit burned a hole in the maze with a small fireball. "That's cheating."

"It's being inventive," she said. "Maybe that's what this maze is all about. You need to think creatively in order to win."

"Hey! You there." A small gnome in a bright red uniform and a matching hat raced toward us.

I groaned. "You've got us in trouble now."

"You don't know that. Maybe she's coming to reward me with a prize for my inventive behavior," Bandit said.

The look on the gnome's face was one of fury. Her cheeks were bright red, and her tiny teeth were exposed. "This is a magical maze. It doesn't respond well to being burned."

"I just wanted to see what was on the other side," Bandit said.

"Not like that, you don't. I'm sure you read the rules outside the maze before coming in," the gnome said.

"There were rules?" Bandit scratched her chin.

"Twelve of them on a large board at the start of the maze," the gnome said. "One of them states that maze contestants cannot cause physical harm to the magical maze."

"Oh, sure. I caught that. It won't happen again," Bandit said.

Her lack of sincerity made the gnome bounce onto her toes and jab a finger in Bandit's belly. It was as high as she could get. "And I'm sure, since you read the rules and understood them, you realize what the punishment is."

Bandit glanced at me. "Patting me on the head and telling me not to do it again?"

"Instant expulsion," the gnome said.

Bandit looked around and chuckled. "Who exactly will expel me from this maze?"

"I am." The gnome grabbed Bandit's leg, and they vanished, leaving a cloud of smoke behind.

I blew out a breath. These maze gnomes didn't mess around. I waited a moment to see if she'd come back for me, but it looked like the gnome was only angry with Bandit.

After pushing aside a few charred branches, I stepped through the burned hole Bandit had made and looked around. There was no one about. I was alone with my muddled thoughts.

I turned in a slow circle, considering which way to go. I could leave, but maybe some quiet time would be a good thing.

I was running out of suspects in Herbert's murder and wasn't any closer to finding the truth. I didn't want to question my dad again. I should go back to Molvos and see if he was hiding something useful. He hadn't been honest about the tests Herbert had run on him. Maybe he was concealing a dark heart inside that little green body.

I turned the corner and stopped. A pixie in a pink and yellow uniform nodded at me and held out a plate with a red cupcake on it.

"Is that for me?" I asked.

"It is. Congratulations, you've reached the cupcake treat stand. I give cupcakes to anyone who finds me." She smiled up at me.

"Thanks." I walked over and took the plate. The cake had a small pink flower nestled on the top of a swirl of white icing. Bandit would be so jealous if she could see me.

"And you look like you need a cupcake, dearie." The pixie patted a small stool before settling on one of her own. "Why don't you take the weight off? I'm excellent with cupcakes, tea, and advice."

I sat on the stool and took a bite of the cupcake. The sweet sponge melted in my mouth, and the icing danced across my tongue with a gentle fizzle. This was no ordinary cupcake.

The pixie tapped me on the knee. "Everything said here is in confidence. The magical maze never spreads gossip. Neither do I."

I finished my cupcake, and she instantly replaced it with another one. It was pale yellow with pink icing and a blue flower. "I've got a problem with a family member."

She pursed her lips and nodded. "Families are often the trickiest. You don't get to choose your family, yet you feel you must stick with them, no matter what they do."

"If I could, I'd choose this family member," I said. "But... well, he doesn't remember me."

Her eyebrows shot up. "A long-lost relative?"

"Something like that," I said. "He's also in trouble. It's serious, and I'm not sure if I can help him. If I don't, I may never get him back to where he belongs."

"People can sometimes be led astray," the pixie said. "This world is full of temptation."

"He wasn't tempted by anything," I said.

"Or they make bad choices."

"He wouldn't do that. Not if he realized how painful it would be for the rest of us."

"Things can happen that mean people do things they don't want to do."

"That could be it. But why do that?" I set my empty plate down. "Why leave everyone you love?"

"Could he be hiding something he's ashamed of?"

Zandra! Her name popped into my head. "It's possible."

"Or maybe he's protecting others. When you really love someone, you do a lot for them. You even sacrifice your own happiness to make sure other people are safe and protected."

"That sounds a lot like the man I remember when I was a kid."

"What does your heart tell you?" the pixie said. "What do you want to happen now you've found this person who's been missing from your life?"

I rested my elbows on my knees. "It's telling me that there's been something missing ever since he disappeared. I have a great family, and I love them all, but there's always been a gap."

"This person would fill that gap?"

"He would," I said. "But the trouble he's in may mean that can never happen."

"You want this person back in your family?"

I nodded without hesitation. "It would make us whole again. It would make our family complete. Everyone misses him, even though we don't talk about him much. I need to help him remember everything he had. I need to get him out of this trouble he's found himself in and take him home with me."

"It sounds as if you have your answer," the pixie said. "You need to do whatever it takes to make that happen."

"He's not a bad man," I said. "He may have done bad things, but he's been changed. The kind, loving person I remember is still in there."

"Then get him back," the pixie said. "I can tell this missing person means a lot to you."

My jaw wobbled, and I bit my bottom lip. "He does."

"Then I wish you all the best on your mission," the pixie said. "Follow your heart. It'll never take you to the wrong place."

"Thanks." I stood and smiled down at the pixie. "That was just what I needed."

She grinned and nodded. "As I said, cupcakes, tea, and advice. Any time you need it, you just find me in the magical maze."

Fortified by cake and the kind words of the pixie, I felt better than I had in days as I retraced my steps out of the magical maze.

I had to believe in my dad. If our roles were reversed, he'd have stood by me no matter what. It didn't matter that we hadn't seen each other for years.

It was time I stood by him. I'd help him figure out this problem and get him home. Where he belonged.

As I emerged from the maze, Bandit was standing beside two unhappy angels. "What did you do?"

She raised her hands. "This isn't a problem of my making."

I arched an eyebrow. "Did the gnome have you arrested for burning a hole in the maze?"

Bandit shook her head. "That's not why the angels are here. Tempest, meet Hadar and Jaron. They're about to blow your mind."

The taller of the two angels glanced at Bandit. "You injured the magical maze? That's a crime."

Bandit waved a hand in the air. "Hadar, that was a minor misdemeanor. Let's focus on the bigger picture."

"And what's the bigger picture?" I asked.

Bandit shook out her wings. "Virginia Lupin's been murdered."

Chapter 16

I stared at Bandit in disbelief before focusing on Hadar. "Who killed Virginia?"

"It was Molvos," Hadar said.

"What? It can't be him. He's in custody, isn't he?"

"He was released less than an hour ago. Molvos finally talked about what happened with Herbert," Hadar said.

"What did he say to make you let him go?" I asked.

The angels exchanged a glance before Hadar continued. "That Abel masterminded everything."

"And you believed him?" I asked. "Did you question Abel? What did he have to say about the accusation?"

The angels exchanged another glance, this one looking less assured.

"Molvos was convincing," the shorter angel, Jaron, said. "He's a reformed character after his treatment."

"And he used to sing to us when we brought him his meals. It was sweet," Hadar said.

I snorted. "Because he sang to you that makes him innocent?"

"Um, no. But he felt remorse because he'd been hiding the truth. He wanted to come clean so the right person went to jail."

"This can't be true," I said. "He accused my da—, I mean, he accused Abel of setting up Herbert's murder, and you didn't question the possibility that he was deflecting attention?"

"Tempest, remember, you may be biased when it comes to Abel," Bandit said quietly.

"I may be biased, but I'm not stupid," I said. "Molvos hated Herbert. He could have killed him. He had the perfect motive to want him dead. He was kidnapped and forced into a series of possibly dangerous experiments. That would make anyone hold a grudge."

Hadar sighed. "We know that now. He fooled us. But there was no physical evidence at the first crime scene. We couldn't hold him any longer even if we wanted to. And when Molvos revealed that Abel Cross was behind what happened to Herbert—"

"Did he actually say that Abel killed Herbert?" I asked.

"No, but apparently, Abel has information that will lead us to the criminal," Jaron said.

"Basically, the angels have messed up big time," Bandit said. "No amount of form filling, stamping, and triple checking the paperwork will fix this disaster."

The angels pouted and fluttered their wings.

"Molvos has been free for an hour and he's killed again," Jaron said.

"Why would he want to kill Virginia?" I asked.

The angels shrugged at the same time, and white downy feathers floated off them and swirled around their heads.

"Maybe he was angry because he'd been captured and held. He took his rage out on the first person he met. He's a dangerous, unstable demon. The sooner Herbert's cure is rolled out, the better. Then there'll be no more crimes like this," Hadar said.

"There'll still be plenty of crime. It's not only demons who mess up." I crossed my arms over my chest. "Let me get this straight. You let Molvos go because of a lack of evidence in the first crime?"

"And his excellent singing voice," Bandit loudly stage whispered.

"We did," Hadar said, after giving Bandit a long stare.

"And he just happened to find Virginia and murder her as soon as he got free?" I shook my head. "How do you know it was Molvos?"

"Several people saw him leaving the crime scene," Jaron said. "He wasn't discreet. His demon bloodlust must have been high. He'd been repressing his natural instincts for days to make us believe he was innocent."

Guilt rattled through me. I should have seen straight through Molvos' cover, but I'd put my personal issues before a crime. My head hadn't been in the game ever since I'd arrived in Puzzlewood. This was the result.

"Where was Virginia killed?" I asked.

"At the house," Jaron said. "It's not a pretty sight. Molvos used his claws to harm her, just like he did on Herbert."

"I'd like to see the body," I said.

"Sophie thought you'd want a look at the crime scene. The authorisation paperwork will take a week to complete."

"We don't have a week. Any evidence will be gone by then, and the killer will have vanished."

"Which is why Sophie's made you a temporary employee of Angel Force."

My jaw dropped. I was a member of the angel gang? I wasn't sure how I felt about that.

"What? No way! Do I get to be an angel, too?" Bandit slapped Hadar on the back.

He staggered forward. "No, just Tempest. And only for twenty-four hours. It was the only thing Sophie could think of to give you access to the site."

"I can handle being a temporary angel. Show me the crime scene."

"Right this way. We'll take you there," Hadar said.

"This isn't looking good for Abel," Bandit muttered as we hurried along behind the angels. "Molvos has basically tattled that he's an accessory to murder."

"This feels wrong. It doesn't make any sense," I said. "What made Molvos change his mind and blab about my dad? He's been in the angels' custody for days. He could have talked and gotten out right away."

"Maybe we've all been deceived by this demon," Bandit said. "He tricked the angels into letting him go free. Maybe that was his grand plan all along. Molvos played the good demon for a while so they'd let their guard down and start looking elsewhere for a suspect. Then he implicated your dad. He got exactly what he wanted."

I sighed. "At least he didn't accuse my dad of killing Herbert. He's innocent of murder."

"The angels may decide to charge him as accessory if he set up Herbert's murder," Bandit said. "He still has a lot to answer for."

We reached the house and headed inside. There were several angels loitering, all of them looking anxious.

"The body is in the bedroom," Hadar said. "If you don't mind, I won't go in. I'm not good with unfortunate situations such as this."

"We'll just take a quick look," I said. I also wasn't great when it came to looking at bodies.

I stepped into the room. Virginia lay on the bed. It looked like she'd fallen backward or been thrown. She was on her back, her arms flung over her head. There were numerous gouges that I didn't spend more than a few seconds looking at that suggested demon claws were involved in her demise.

It looked like a classic demon attack. Messy, chaotic, and brutal.

Bandit leaned against the door, watching me as I walked around the room. "Anything of interest?"

"Nothing looks out of place," I said.

"So, it was Molvos if those marks are anything to go by," Bandit said.

"Or a mystery demon we've yet to meet." I headed out of the room and back to the angels. "Have you arrested Molvos and asked why he did this?"

"He's on the run," Jaron said. "He was last seen heading to the border. There's a group of angels tracking him."

"Then let's go catch our killer." I headed out of the house with Bandit, accompanied by Hadar, who directed us to the last known sighting of Molvos.

"I can't leave my post," Hadar said as he backed into the house. "Sophie asked us to find you, but then we were to come back here. Head toward the border in the east and you'll soon spot the angels."

"Thanks," I said.

"I'll fly us to the border," Bandit said. "It'll be quicker, and you'll be able to see more when we're on the wing."

Although I wasn't a fan of being flown anywhere by Bandit, she had a point.

"On three," she said, "One, two, th—"

"Wait a second. I see something." I yanked my arm out of her grasp. "Isn't that Molvos?"

Bandit stepped past me and squinted. "Huh! It looks like him. But he's supposed to be trying to escape through the border. This is the center of town."

"Let's follow him." I dashed along the lane, my attention on the short green demon who hurried along with his head down. He was being careful not to draw attention to himself, and I couldn't get a good look at his face. But from the back, it looked just like our lying demon.

I ran along with Bandit beside me and turned the corner.

"There he is." Bandit pointed ahead as the demon turned another corner in front of us. "I'm certain that's him now we're closer."

"So am I. But he sure is fast for a little guy," I said.

"We're faster." Bandit grabbed my collar and yanked me into the air as she took flight.

It felt like I'd left my stomach behind as we shot over the rooftops and landed in the spot we'd seen Molvos a few seconds ago. "Jeez! Give a girl a warning before you do that."

Bandit grinned as she let go of my collar. "You should be thanking me. Not everyone gets a chance to fly with the fairies."

"Lucky me." I rounded the corner and slammed into a short white-haired woman.

She gave a cry of alarm as she bounced off me.

"Mrs. Winkler?" I was already kneeling over her as she lay on the ground moaning. "I'm so sorry. I didn't see you."

"And I didn't see you, my dear. You appeared out of nowhere."

"Yes, I suppose we did." I touched her arm gently, feeling nothing but skin and bone. "You aren't hurt?"

She tried to sit, and the color drained from her face. "My hip. I think it's badly bruised."

"Let me help you," I said. "You may feel better once you're on your feet."

I tried to get her sitting, but she cried out again. "Oh, dear. I'm not sure I can get up. Something feels wrong. I have a stabbing pain in my hip that gets worse when I move."

I'd slammed into her so hard, it was a wonder she wasn't unconscious. "Bandit, you'd better take Mrs. Winkler to get medical help."

"What about Molvos?" Bandit said. "We almost had him. If we hurry, we can still snatch him before he gets too far."

"Molvos? I thought that demon was in custody?" Mrs. Winkler's pale face turned from me to Bandit. "Has he escaped?"

"No, but there's been a development in the case," I said. "Don't worry about that right now. You need help. Bandit will take you to be looked after. You just focus on getting better."

Her tongue poked out between her teeth as she touched her hip and hissed out a breath. "Maybe I should see a doctor. I have brittle bones. I was diagnosed just last year. No amount of magic has helped me yet. Old age gets to the best of us."

Eek! I could have shattered this sweet old lady with my clumsiness.

"Handle Mrs. Winkler carefully," I said to Bandit. She'd better not shoot in the air like a jack-in-the-box or the shock might kill her.

Bandit scooped up Mrs. Winkler, cradling her like a child against her chest. "I can be careful when I need to be. I'll catch up with you once I've dropped her at the hospital." She launched into the air and vanished out of sight.

I might have heard a terrified scream from Mrs. Winkler, but there was nothing I could do for her now. Trust in the crazy fairy, that was the best I could offer. At least she'd get to the hospital quickly and get treated.

I hunted along the street for several minutes, but Molvos had escaped me. I retraced my steps to where I'd rammed into Mrs. Winkler, but it was no use. I'd lost the trail. Molvos had slipped away.

With a growl of annoyance, I kicked at a loose stone before making my way toward the border.

A group of angels were huddled around something as I approached.

"We've got him," one of them yelled.

I sped up. She couldn't mean Molvos. But there he was, surrounded by angels. He really could move fast. He'd gotten halfway across Puzzlewood in minutes and didn't even look out of breath. Although he did look furious and confused to find himself pinned by a troop of excited angels, their wings fluttering and feathers floating in all directions.

My dad stood to one side, watching the angels, a scowl on his stubbled face.

I marched over to him. "What are you doing here?"

He shrugged, his gaze flicking to me before shifting back to the angels. "Watching the angels make a big mistake."

"There's no mistake this time. Molvos just killed Virginia Lupin. And he's trying to take you down with him for Herbert's murder."

"That's not possible."

"That he's a killer, or he's implicating you for Herbert's murder?"

"Both. Molvos was talking to me ten minutes ago."

"How do you know when Virginia was killed?"

"People gossip. Besides, you just told me."

"Why are you giving Molvos an alibi?" I crossed my arms over my chest. "And how come you haven't been arrested by the angels? Molvos told them you're neck deep in setting up Herbert's murder."

"I'm not bothered if he did. They have no proof to make that claim stick. And they're only interested in Molvos right now. Have you noticed how single-minded angels can be? Besides, why would they want me? I'm innocent in all of this."

"You're not innocent of cheating on your family," I muttered.

He straightened and glared at me. "What was that?"

"Nothing," I said.

"No, spit it out. Ever since we met in the bar, you've had a problem with me. What's your deal?"

I glared at him, anger and frustration simmering through me. "What if I do have a problem?"

"Tempest, great news." Sophie raced over, a bright smile on her face. "We've captured Molvos. We finally have our killer. Did you see? My angels got him. I can't believe it. I mean, I can, of course. They're super at their jobs. But this will be a feather in everyone's cap."

"You're wrong." My dad glared at me before turning his attention to Sophie, who took a step back. "I'll vouch for him. Molvos may be a snitch, but he's my snitch. He was with me when that woman was killed. He couldn't have murdered her."

Sophie cleared her throat and glanced at me. "I'm sorry to say, Mr. Cross, your word isn't worth much around here. You've provided an alibi for Molvos before, and he's just shown himself to be a ruthless killer."

"He didn't do this." My dad's hands clenched into fists. "You've got the wrong demon."

"So, who did it if it wasn't him?" I asked.

My dad simply smirked.

"We've got our demon," Sophie said. "I'm certain of it. And I shall be speaking to you about your involvement in Professor Winkler's unfortunate incident, Mr. Cross."

"I may be hard to find. And if you're going to pin that on me, you can think again," he said.

Sophie's lips pursed, and the flush on her cheeks faded. "I should have trusted my first instincts. If I had, Molvos would never have been free, and Virginia would still be alive."

"No, she wouldn't," my dad said. "At least, she wouldn't be dead by Molvos' claws."

"You tell them, Abel," Molvos yelled as the angels led him away.

"I've got your back," my dad said, his ice-cold gaze fixed on the group of angels.

Molvos looked at me and cupped his hands together. "Help me. I didn't do this. I wasn't even there."

I didn't know what to say that would help him. There were witnesses that had seen Molvos leaving the house. And, as much as I hated to admit it, Sophie had a point. My dad's alibi couldn't be relied on. He wasn't reliable.

"We need to process the paperwork, and then we can formally charge Molvos," Sophie said, her radiant smile returning. "But we've done it. This case is solved." She patted my arm before trotting away after her angels.

"This isn't right," my dad said, his voice a low growl in his throat.

"Why do you care?" I asked. "You're a tough bounty hunter who only looks out for himself."

"You got that right." He raked a hand through his hair. "But Molvos doesn't deserve this. Come on. I'm not done with you yet." He strode after the angels, not looking back to see if I'd follow him.

"What's that supposed to mean?" I hurried along beside him.

"We have unfinished business." He slid me a glance. "You've got a problem with me, and I need to know what it is. I don't need some angry witch hounding me. I have enough to deal with."

I pressed my lips together. It felt like truth time. My dad needed to know about his real family.

"Great. Now I get the silent treatment." He shook his head.

"I'm not silent, just thinking." I had to figure out how to tell him who he really was and get him to believe me.

"When you're done thinking, you let me know. Then we can finish this and get on with our lives." He slowed and glared at me. "And just to be clear, I don't plan to have you in my life for much longer. I ride solo. Always have."

"Is that so? You sure about that?"

Confusion flickered in his eyes before the coldness returned. "Yeah. I'll be glad when you're gone. I don't plan on seeing you again."

I ran my tongue over my teeth. If that's what he really wanted, he'd be disappointed. Now I'd found him, I was never letting go.

Chapter 17

The sun dipped below the horizon as I paced around the reception area in the Angel Force building.

My dad looked like he was asleep, his feet kicked up on a chair and his eyes closed.

Bandit strolled in through the door, a brown paper bag in her hand. "Bow down before me, weaklings. I come bearing treats." She sat in the seat next to my dad. "Anyone for some pecan pie? I put it on your tab at the cafe, Tempest."

"I have a tab?"

"You do now."

"Get out of my personal space, fairy," my dad muttered, his eyes remaining shut. "If you get glitter on my jacket, I'm yanking your wings off."

"That's not very friendly," Bandit said. "Have some pie. It might cheer you up." She held a piece of pie under his nose.

He pushed her hand away. "The only thing that'll cheer me up is when those angels admit they've made a mistake. Why won't they listen to me?"

"Because you're never honest with them," I said. "You cause them problems when you come to town.

You take money from anyone who'll pay you and do jobs that most people with a conscience turn down."

He opened one eye. "Have you got a copy of my resume tucked in your back pocket?"

I tutted and kept pacing.

"We can't all have happy carefree lives like you do," he said.

"My life isn't carefree," I said. "You know that."

"That's the thing. I know nothing about you." He opened his other eye and placed his feet on the floor. "You act like I know your whole history. You're just some grumpy witch who strolled into my favorite bar a few days ago and started jabbing at me. I still can't figure out what you want. And you don't seem to want to tell me."

Bandit raised her eyebrows as she ate a piece of pie. "Is this a bonding moment? Should I leave the room?"

"No. How's Mrs. Winkler doing?" I asked her.

"I checked in at the hospital after getting the pie," Bandit said. "She's fractured her hip."

I winced. "That sounds bad. I didn't mean to run into her."

"The doctor think she'll be okay. She's responding to treatment and healing spells. She kept asking what was going on with Herbert."

"What did you tell her?"

"Not much. I didn't want to give her false hope that justice was about to be served. The angels still don't know what happened to Herbert." She turned to my dad. "However, I know a man who might. Care to share?"

"Keep eating your pie, fairy. I'm saying nothing," my dad said.

The door behind the reception desk opened. Sophie stepped out and gestured me over.

"What's going on back there?" I peered over her shoulder.

"We've been speaking to Molvos," Sophie said, a line of tension on her forehead. "He's not being helpful."

"And he won't be helpful if you're trying to frame him for this murder." My dad stood and strode over. "Let that demon go. He's innocent."

Sophie glanced at Abel and frowned. "We don't think he is. Tempest, we could do with your help to get him to talk. Your experience with demons will be invaluable."

"What's this witch got to do with demons?" my dad asked.

"The Crypt family is renowned for their experience with demons," Sophie said. "They've been successfully protecting the world from demons for centuries."

His hand went to his forehead. "Crypt witches? Why is that name so familiar?"

My head shot around, and I stared at him. "You know us?"

He swayed on his feet. "I know something about you. You reckon you're some kind of great demon hunter?"

"She's the best." Bandit walked over and draped an arm around my shoulders. "You really should take the time to get to know her better. I reckon you'll have a heap of things in common. You may even like her. She grows on you like a delightful fungus on the side of a tree. Squishy, sort of odd looking, but you can't seem to stop staring at her."

"I can make my own opinions about people." My dad pointed a finger at Sophie. "Molvos was with me when Virginia was killed. He can't be in two places at once. You've got the wrong demon."

My mouth twisted to the side. Or could he? I'd been surprised at how quickly Molvos had gotten away and made it to the border. Had he really been able to move that quickly, or was magic involved?

"Molvos is ready to be interviewed by you," Sophie said, keeping her gaze fixed on me.

I went to follow Sophie, but my dad grabbed my arm.

"We're not done," he said.

I let out a slow breath. "I know. We've got a lot to talk about."

He let go of my arm and rolled his shoulders. "I don't know. There's something about you that sets me on edge. I need to figure out what that is."

I chewed on my bottom lip. "What do you suggest we do about that?"

"I suppose you leaving town and never coming back is not an option you'd go for?"

I snorted out air. "Well worked out."

"I figured as much. Let's meet later. I'm done wasting time with these angels. We can grab something to eat, and you can tell me what your issue is."

I nodded. This felt like a breakthrough. If I could get Dad on his own and make him open up, that could be the way in I needed. It might jog his memory.

I wanted to jump up and down and hug him, but playing it cool was required. "Fine. Where do you want to meet?"

"Pedro's Pizza Parlor over on Cinnamon Street. I'll see you there in an hour."

Hope fluttered through me as he walked away. I was getting somewhere with my dad. But first, I had to tackle Molvos.

I headed to the interview room with Sophie. Molvos was sitting at a table when I entered, his head down.

He lifted his head, sadness glinting in his eyes. "Please make the angels believe that I didn't do this."

I settled in the seat opposite him, while Sophie remained by the door. My thoughts flicked to the conversation with my dad. He'd sensed something between us. I just knew it. I pushed the thoughts away. Solve this murder first, then fix my family.

"Let's start with Herbert's murder before we get on to Virginia. You didn't tell the truth when we spoke about your relationship with him," I said. "How did you come to be in his experiments?"

Molvos tapped his claws on the table. "I may have concealed some facts, but I didn't lie. I came to respect Professor Winkler."

"Not to begin with?"

"No, I wasn't truthful about how I got onto his trial. I didn't volunteer. Professor Winkler was struggling to find demons to take part. He got desperate and began trapping us."

"Which gives you the perfect motive for wanting him dead," I said. "He held you prisoner whilst he experimented on you."

Sophie gasped softly. "Is this true?"

Molvos nodded. "He did. At first, I was raging mad. I'd been a happy-go-lucky demon, content with causing chaos and not caring about the consequences. I didn't realize how empty and meaningless my life was until Professor Winkler stepped in and showed me there was a different way. A better way to live."

"You wanted revenge because Herbert kidnapped you and forced you to go through these experiments," I said.

"I understand that it doesn't look good for me," Molvos said. "And for the first few months of the trials, I thought a lot about how I'd like to kill him. I used to dream about seeing him dead on the floor. Then something changed. I no longer felt rage. I began to look forward to the tests. I felt a peace I'd never experienced before. It was joyful. I wanted more."

"Only because your ability was suppressed by whatever Herbert pumped you full of. It isn't a cure. It didn't stop you from being a demon."

"You're wrong. But it was more than that," Molvos said. "Professor Winkler spoke to me like I was his equal. He never considered me less because of the dark deeds I'd done."

"It sounds like you have Stockholm Syndrome," I said. "You began to like your captor. You formed a bond with him."

"Maybe I did. But it was because of the cure," Molvos said. "I changed. I became a better demon. A better non-demon."

"Did you also not tell the truth about your whereabouts when Herbert was murdered?" I asked.

"I was truthful about that. I spent most of the evening with Abel in the bar. It was just bad luck that I was close to the scene of the crime, got spotted by Saul, and ran into an angel. But that's it. The angels will confirm there was no physical evidence to put me at the scene."

I glanced at Sophie, and she nodded. "It was one of the reasons we released him."

"Let's move on to Virginia," I said. "You were released from custody, and she winds up dead an hour later."

"That is another horrible coincidence," Molvos said.

"You were seen again," I said. I looked over at Sophie. "Are the witnesses reliable?"

"They are," Sophie said. "Three people saw Molvos leaving the house just before Virginia was discovered."

"I didn't do that. I wasn't even there. I was with Abel again. I know he's told you that. Why would he lie?" Molvos gripped the edge of the table.

"Because he doesn't want his accomplice behind bars," Sophie said.

"I'm not important to Abel," Molvos said. "I like to think I am, but he barely tolerates me hanging around him. I annoy him. There's no reason he'd be my alibi and cover for me."

"What were you and Abel doing together?" I asked.

"We went drinking, same as most days. I planned to celebrate my release."

"Did anyone see you together?" I asked.

"Yes! The barman did." Molvos bounced in his seat. "He'll confirm we were there and what time we left. Probably. I mean, he drinks a lot, but he's a decent guy."

"Has this been checked?" I asked Sophie.

"My angels are over there now," she said. "That barman isn't a reliable witness, though. As Molvos said, he drinks too much of his stock to be relied on. He once reported he saw a black unicorn flying over Puzzlewood being ridden by a witch. Everyone knows there is no such thing as black unicorns."

"He may like a drink, but he's a good guy," Molvos said. "He alerted me that the angels wanted to talk to me about Virginia's murder."

"He helped you escape?" I asked.

"No! Hold on now. I never said that. I don't want any trouble for him," Molvos said, his gaze flitting between me and Sophie. "He simply gave me a useful piece of information. He didn't tell me what to do with it. I was the one who made a run for it."

"Why do that? It suggests guilt not innocence," I said.

Molvos hung his head. "Yeah, not my smartest of moves, but I panicked. I knew this would happen. The angels were gunning for me. I needed breathing space, a chance to think and get everything sorted."

"Are you any good at translocation spells?" I asked.

"Nah, they're not in my wheelhouse," he said. "I've never been good at big spells like that. I find it hard to focus. I get by on these little legs and my charming personality. Why do you ask?"

"Because I saw you," I said. "I'd just been to the crime scene to see what you'd done to Virginia—"

"I did nothing to her."

"Fine. What you allegedly did to her. When I left the house, you were in the center of Puzzlewood. You were in a hurry and didn't want people to notice you. You were running from something."

"That can't be right." Sophie approached the table. "Are you sure it was Molvos?"

"I was surprised to see him, but it was him," I said. "And since you don't normally allow demons into Puzzlewood, I figured it had to be Molvos."

She shook her head. "My angels had him in their sights the whole time. They tracked his movements to the border. He couldn't have been back at the house. One of my angels was always following him."

"I'm telling you it was him," I said. "I tracked him with Bandit."

"Do you have a twin?" Sophie asked. "Have you snuck a relative into Puzzlewood without informing me?"

He chuckled. It stopped quickly. "Oh! You're not joking. No! I have no twin. That wasn't me you saw," Molvos said. "I was making a run for it straight to the border. I figured, if I got out of Puzzlewood, I'd be able to hide, keep my head down until this blew over and the angels figured out their mistake."

I shifted in my seat. Something felt wrong here. Either there were two Molvos' or I'd tracked the wrong demon.

"Molvos, you claim to be a reformed demon. Why don't you make it easy on everyone and confess?" Sophie said. "Surely you want a clear conscience. Virginia didn't deserve to die."

"Which is why I didn't kill her," Molvos said. "I liked Virginia. She was often around when I was having my treatment. She was kind to me. I often got snacks off her. I had no problem with her. And I also had no problem with Professor Winkler. I'm not confessing to anything, because I didn't do it. I didn't kill either of them."

I sat back in my seat. He sounded convincing. And there was a niggle at the back of my head that wouldn't stay quiet.

Two sightings of Molvos in different places at the same time. That couldn't be explained. Add to that my dad was defending Molvos and offering him an alibi when he could have kept quiet, and I had a problem.

I knew my dad. He'd had a passion for defending people and helping the innocent when they were accused of something they didn't do. He always supported righteousness and made sure justice was done.

I was missing something, but I couldn't figure out what it was.

"Perhaps we need to take a break," Sophie said. "Molvos, your cell is waiting for you. And we'll have the test results back soon from the scrapings taken from your claws. That should settle this matter."

"You won't find anything that links me to the murder," he said. "And when there's no evidence that I was anywhere near Virginia, what will you do then?"

He had an excellent point. I pushed back my chair and stood. "Let me know when the test results come in."

"Of course," Sophie said as she followed me to the door. "Thanks for your help, Tempest. I have a good feeling about this. We can close these dreadful cases and move on."

I nodded as I headed out the door with her. Somehow, I didn't think it would be that simple.

Chapter 18

"Are you sure you don't want me to come to dinner with you?" Bandit stood beside me as we waited outside the pizza parlor for my dad to arrive.

"I need to do this on my own," I said.

"What if Abel turns nasty?" Bandit's gaze was on the menu inside the window. "I could grab my own table, you could treat me to a large stuffed crust with a side order of garlic bread, and I could keep an eye on the situation."

"No. You'll get distracted by the food."

"As if. You're really going to reveal that you're his daughter?"

"No. I don't know. Not right away, anyway. But he reacted when he heard my full name. My real dad is in there. I'm going to drop a few hints and see how he responds. I'm getting through. I just know it."

She glanced at me out of the corner of her eye. "You don't think that's wishful thinking?"

"Nope."

"Hey. I didn't think you'd come." My dad strode toward us, his hands stuffed into his jeans pockets.

"I said I'd be here."

His gaze flicked to Bandit. "The fairy's coming too?"

"I will if you don't behave yourself." Bandit expanded her wings as she glared at my dad.

He lifted a hand. "I'll be on my best behavior. But we need to talk, and I don't like the company you keep."

"My company is excellent." Bandit loomed over him.

I eased myself between them. "I'll catch up with you later, Bandit."

She shrugged before walking away. "It's your funeral."

"What's that supposed to mean?" my dad asked.

"Ignore her. She's annoyed because she's not getting a free pizza out of me."

He rocked back on his heels before nodding then pulled open the door and gestured me to go in.

I headed inside and got an instant hit of warm melted cheese, garlic, and basil.

My dad lifted a hand to a guy behind the counter as he led me through to the back of the pizza parlor. We settled at a small table out of earshot of anyone else.

"You like pizza?" I asked.

"There's no better food," he said.

"You've been here before?"

"I've lost count of the number of times."

"What do you recommend?" I studied the menu as my stomach did somersaults. It was so weird being alone with my dad when he didn't know who I was. This used to be a normal everyday thing for us, going out to grab a slice of pizza. I didn't realize how badly I'd missed it until now.

"It's all good. This is the best pizza parlor in Puzzlewood. I recommend the Bismarck. It comes with ham and a fried egg on top."

I wrinkled my nose. "Interesting."

He chuckled. "It's not for everyone."

"I'll go for the Romana."

"Anchovies. Nasty. I won't try any of yours."

The waitress came over and took our order before walking away.

My dad stared at me in silence for a few seconds. "You behave like you know me. Have we met before?"

"Before I answer that, why don't you tell me about your daughter?" I wasn't quite ready to reveal all. Baby steps were needed, and my courage had raced away for now.

"Zandra?" Surprise flashed across his face.

"You do have a daughter?"

"Sure. You can't be friends with her, though. And I don't figure you as a teacher. Exactly how do you know my daughter?" His gaze narrowed a fraction as he laid his hands flat on the table.

"I never said I knew her," I said. "How old is she?"

"Eight," he said. "What's it to you?"

I sucked in a breath. "You don't strike me as a family man. I'm trying to figure out what makes you tick."

"Then leave my daughter out of it," he said. "She's got nothing to do with you."

She had everything to do with me. "Do you see her often?"

"I see her enough," he said. "She lives with her mom since I don't have a permanent base. Whenever I'm here, I make sure she visits. She's a good kid. I can't believe she's mine."

"You're not with her mom?"

"It didn't work out," he said. "She figured she wanted a bad boy. When she realized just how bad I was, she didn't stick around. By then, she was pregnant with Zandra. I see them both right. Zandra gets everything she needs."

"Apart from her dad being in her life all the time," I said.

He grunted. "It's better that way."

"Have you got a picture of her?"

Those familiar eyes narrowed again. "Of course."

"May I see it?"

He reached into his back pocket and pulled out his wallet before flipping it open. A smiling, dark-haired girl with a cute button nose grinned back at me from a small picture.

"She looks happy."

"Zandra's a good kid." He looked at the photo and rubbed his thumb over it. "You know, you kinda look like her."

My throat tightened. "There is a resemblance. Funny that."

His bottom lip jutted out as he put his wallet away. "You sound like you know how that feels, not having a dad around all the time. Where's your dad? Ditched you for an easy life?"

I swallowed the answer I longed to give. "No, he's close by. He's a great guy. He was always there when I was growing up."

"You're an only child?"

"I have a sister. Her name's Aurora."

"Nice name," he said.

He would think that. He chose it after she was born. "She's great. Lots of fun to be around. She runs a magic store in Willow Tree Falls. Have you heard of it?"

"Sure. Everyone knows about that place. You've got that enormous stone circle. And all the tourists flock there to use the hot springs, don't they?"

"That's right. Ever been?"

His head tilted, and something flashed in his eyes. "Can't say I have. Why the interest in my kid and my travels?"

"Um, just curious."

"I get the impression you get curious about a lot of things. That could get a person in trouble."

We were quiet as the waitress returned with our pizzas and drinks.

I used the food as an excuse to grab my scattered thoughts together. Everything I wanted to say to him was on the tip of my tongue, but I just couldn't blurt it out.

"So, you still haven't said what your problem is with me." He bit into his pizza.

My insides felt like they were being shaken. I placed a hand on my stomach and took a deep breath. "Have you ever heard the name Artie Crypt?"

My dad shuddered in his seat, and his eyes fluttered closed. "I... I'm not sure. Who is he?"

I swallowed, my mouth dryer than the Sahara. "He's my dad."

He started to nod, then his head shifted from side to side. "I can't say I've run into the guy."

A lick of heat ran up my spine. I clutched the edge of the table and squeezed my eyes shut. That felt like Frank stirring. He hadn't reacted for months. Was he concerned that I was about to break through my dad's barriers?

I forced myself to relax. I reached across the table to touch the back of my dad's hand.

He yanked it away, and his eyes narrowed. "What is it with you? You look at me as if I'm supposed to solve your problems. I only do that if you pay me enough money. Is that what this is about? You have a job for me?"

I dropped my gaze. "It's not that. Although maybe you can solve my problems."

He pushed back his seat. "You're crazy. This was a mistake. I don't know why I asked you here."

I tensed, my fingers clenching and my heart thundering. "Wait! Don't go."

"Give me one good reason why I should stay."

"Because... I think you need my help. And I know I need yours."

He blew out a breath. "We can't help each other. And I need nothing from you."

"I can help with Molvos."

His nostrils flared, but then he nodded and grabbed a slice of pizza before pulling his seat back in.

I let out a sigh. Maybe I'd pushed too far, but he'd reacted. When I'd said the name Artie Crypt, something had shifted inside him. And Frank had also reacted. This was progress.

"Let's finish the pizza," I said, my heart bouncing in my chest like it wanted to burst. "It's really good."

His gaze went to his plate, and he hunched over it, stuffing the pizza into his mouth as he avoided eye contact with me.

My appetite was gone, but I took a bite of pizza, anyway. "Where did you grow up?"

One shoulder lifted. "We moved around a lot. Nowhere stuck for long."

That wasn't true. I knew all about his childhood. "Are your parents still alive?"

He glanced up, his forehead wrinkled. "I don't think about them."

That was a weird response. Everyone thought about their family, even if they weren't close. "Where did you go to school?"

"Stop with the questions. Like I said, we moved around a lot. I don't really remember that time."

I ate another bite of pizza without tasting it. Was that true, or did Dad have no memory older than ten years? Since the time he left Willow Tree Falls, had his past been wiped away?

"What about old friends? Do you stay in touch?"

He threw down his pizza. "What is this, twenty questions? I don't think about the past. There's no point dwelling on it. I focus on the present. That's all that matters."

"No plans for the future?" I asked. "Not even with your daughter?"

"That's it. I've had enough. You're worse than the angels with the questions and prodding."

I lifted a hand as color rose on my dad's cheeks. "How about we stick with murder as a conversation topic?"

"There'll be more murder if you keep testing me."

I shook my head. "You'd never hurt me."

"Don't bet on it, kid."

I would. This was my dad, the one guy I could rely on for anything. "You're convinced Molvos is innocent of Herbert's murder."

"Yep," he said after a few seconds of glaring at me. "And I'm not covering for him when it comes to Virginia."

I sat forward in my seat. "It's so strange. I was sure I was chasing Molvos. I'd left the crime scene with Bandit when we saw him near the house where Virginia was killed. But when I caught up with the angels, they had him surrounded."

"Okay, that is odd. Do you think he's innocent?"

I nodded. "I do. And he has no motive for killing Virginia. Herbert, I get. I found out how he mistreated him during the trial phase of the demon cure."

"Which is another big mistake."

"You don't approve of the work on the cure?"

"No. If there are no demons, there won't be much work for either of us." A smile flickered across his face. "And you can't approve, since you're supposed to be this mad, bad demon catcher."

"That's a fair point. Although, I don't just catch them. I also swallow them when I have to."

He blinked, and there was another spark of something close to recognition in his eyes. "You don't say. That's a rare gift."

"Not everyone thinks it's a gift. And gulping down a demon will never taste like marshmallow sundaes."

"I imagine not." His gaze ran over me as he slowly nodded. "You are full of surprises."

"We both are." I shrugged. "Just don't tell me you killed Herbert so you'd still have plenty of work."

"Hah! If you want to use that motive on me, I'll throw it right back at you."

I risked a grin, which he sort of returned.

He leaned back in his seat. "Molvos is sly. That's why I like him, but he isn't involved in this."

"Since the angels won't take your word on that, what's our next move?"

"*Our* next move?"

I pulled a piece off my paper napkin. "He's your friend, and I want to make sure the real killer is brought to justice, so, yes. Why don't we work together on this?"

"What about that enormous fairy you hang out with? Isn't she your sidekick?"

"She's not here to solve a mystery," I said. "Bandit is my bodyguard because my sister insisted upon it. She's more interested in the water park and brownies than anything else."

He gave another shrug. "I can handle a short-term partner. Note the emphasis on short-term."

"I wouldn't want to cramp your style."

That earned me a smirk. "Show me the site where you saw Molvos. We can start there. You could have missed something."

I couldn't help but smile. I was getting through to him. "Great. We can go now if you're not busy."

"Fine by me."

Dad paid for the food at the counter before we headed out of the pizza parlor.

I tried hard to play it cool and not keep smiling. Even if we didn't turn up anything new in this investigation, I got to spend more time with my dad.

We could have a breakthrough of our own tonight.

Chapter 19

"He was heading away from the house where Virginia was killed," I said as I showed my dad where I'd seen Molvos. "He was hurrying, keeping his head down as if he didn't want to be seen."

My dad simply grunted as we walked along the quiet streets. It was getting late, and there weren't many other people around.

"He doesn't live out this way," he said. "And as far as I know, he doesn't have any associates around here. What was he up to skulking about this place?"

"Where does this lane lead if he'd kept going?"

"There's staff accommodation that way, but it's basically a path into the forest. Molvos likes the town scene. He doesn't like nature. This is out of character for him."

"Maybe he was trying to remain undetected by the angels," I said.

"If he wanted to do that, he'd go underground, not into the trees."

"When I interviewed him, Molvos said he couldn't do translocation spells. Is that true?"

"He wasn't lying. He doesn't use that kind of magic. He's more hands-on. He's good at deception and stealing things. It's a handy skill. I don't think he has the power to use translocation magic." He glanced at me. "How about you?"

"What do you mean?"

"The angels keep on about how you're some great demon hunter. That's got to come with power. What are we talking about?"

"You don't know the half of it." I rested a hand briefly over my heart.

His gaze ran over me. "I have a feeling I do. I still don't know how I know you, but I keep getting these weird glimpses in my head. You have a dog, don't you?"

My breath left my body in a big whoosh. "How do you know that?"

He scratched the stubble on his chin. "No idea. I just do."

"His name is Wiggles," I said. "Do you remember that?"

"Nope. Maybe I read about you somewhere," he said. "If you're as good as everyone reckons you are when it comes to demons, you must be famous in the magic community."

"The Crypt family is well-known for their ability with demons," I said. "But I'm not one to give interviews. I keep a low profile. If the demons don't know what I look like, it makes it easier to track them."

"Smart thinking," he said.

"I was raised by smart parents," I said. "They encouraged me to try my hardest and refine my ability."

"Good for them."

"I bet you do the same with your daughter," I said. "When you spoke about Zandra, I could tell how proud you were."

"She's the only good thing I've ever done in my life," he said. "Of course, I'm going to be proud."

I swallowed the lump in my throat. It was so hard not to blurt out everything. He had so much to look forward to; he just needed to remember.

"What happened after you lost Molvos?" he asked.

"We ran into Herbert's mom. I literally knocked her off her feet. She's in the hospital with a fractured hip."

His gaze ran over the ground. "Where did that happen?"

"Just up here." I led him along the lane, rounded the corner and stopped.

Dad pulled a vial of red liquid from his pocket, took out the cap, and sprinkled it around.

"What's that for?" I asked.

"I've got a few skills of my own," he said. "I know people who are happy to trade spells for my particular kind of favors. This is a reveal potion. It'll show us if there was any magic used by this demon you tracked. It could give us a lead on who he is and his abilities."

A smile lifted the corner of my mouth. Dad had always been like this. He loved poking around and asking questions. And he'd always prod me for answers and make me think beyond the obvious. I got my ability to see things other people missed from him.

"What's with the grin?" He glanced at me.

"Just remembering something that makes me happy," I said. "That's a good use of this spell. I wouldn't have thought about trying it."

"I bet you would, given enough time." He knelt and pointed at the ground. "What do you think this is?"

At first, I couldn't see anything. I crouched beside him. There were a few tiny specks of something sparkly in what looked like glue.

I reached out to touch it, but he slapped my hand away.

"Let me. Whatever this is, it isn't natural." He swiped his finger over the goo.

I wrinkled my nose. "That could be anything. Make sure to wash your hands after—"

He reared back, hissing in what must be pain and clutching his hand to his chest.

I leaped up and grabbed hold of him. "What's wrong? What happened? Are you hurt?" My eyes widened as I stared at his hand. Or what was once his hand. My dad had a huge elongated finger with a claw at the end.

"That spell stung like a hornet on steroids." He shook his hand as if trying to dislodge his new claw.

I touched the claw. My hand tingled, and a wash of ice cold followed by blazing heat shot across my palm. A second later, it was covered in dull green scales.

I lifted my hand and stared at it. "That wasn't a magic spell you touched. It was shapeshifter residue."

"No kidding," he said.

"The angels let shapeshifters in?"

"Nope. There shouldn't be any in Puzzlewood. Having them around is too much trouble." He flexed his long claw finger. "You never know who you're speaking to when you have shapeshifters around."

I ran my fingers over the rough scales on my skin. "We've got one on the loose now."

"And we're not talking your average werewolf shifter," he said. "They just leave fur and shredded clothes behind."

"This magic user has the skill to alter their form into whatever they want." I looked from the claw to my new scales. "Whoever it is, they made Molvos the fall guy for murder. Someone used their shifting ability to look like Molvos. That's why he was in two places at once."

Dad grunted in response.

"Does your new claw hurt?" I asked.

"It stings. Nothing I can't handle."

"It won't last for long," I said. "There was only a tiny amount of magic left behind in that goo. My scales are already fading."

"Shapeshifter magic is powerful stuff, but any fool with money can buy that ability temporarily. We may not be looking for a full-on shapeshifter."

"Just someone with a massive grudge against Herbert and a problem with Virginia," I said, "maybe someone who was following him while he was on tour."

"You're thinking a demon who hates the idea of a cure?"

"Possibly. Although a demon wouldn't waste their time using shapeshifter magic to disguise themselves. It's too sneaky. They're more slash and burn. It has to be someone else."

"What about Herbert's mom?"

My eyebrows shot up. "Mrs. Winkler? She's a sweet little old lady. She wouldn't hurt a fly."

"Yet she was right here just when you thought you were chasing Molvos." He waggled the claw on the end of his finger. "What was she doing here, anyway?"

"I didn't think to ask," I said. "It can't be her."

"It can if she isn't really an innocent little old lady."

"But... she's Herbert's mom. Why would she want to kill him?"

"That's something you need to ask her face to face," he said.

The scales faded from my skin as I replayed the possibility that Herbert's own mother had something to do with his death. "Herbert and Virginia used to date. Maybe his mom didn't like their relationship. That can't be it, though. They weren't together."

Dad tapped my forehead with his finger. "Less thinking and more action. That always works for me."

I nodded. We needed to get to the hospital and discover if Mrs. Winkler was a murdering shapeshifter disguised as a sweet old lady.

Chapter 20

"Hold up." I pulled up outside of my dad's favorite bar as we dashed toward the hospital.

"Problem?" he asked.

"I need to let the angels know what's going on."

"Do that. And tell them to let Molvos go while you're at it."

I pulled open the door to the bar. "I'll ask Sophie to bring Molvos to the hospital. If we confront Herbert's mom while he's there, she may think we've discovered the truth about her and let something slip."

"An innocent little old lady's word against a twisted, devious demon." My dad smirked and shook his head. "Good luck with that. I'd put money on who the angels will believe."

"Don't be so sure about that," I said. "The angels want to see the right person arrested for these murders as much as we do."

I raced into the bar, paid to use the snow globe, and contacted Sophie before giving her an update about what we'd discovered.

"You're certain about this, Tempest?" The concern in her voice was clear. "How can you trust Abel?"

"I wish I could explain it to you, but he's onto something. That goo we found had shapeshifter qualities. And that shapeshifter is involved in these murders."

"I don't know how one managed to slip through our defenses."

"Worry about that another time. Let's get Molvos and Mrs. Winkler together and see what happens."

"I still can't believe Mrs. Winkler is involved," Sophie said.

"I know it's a shocker. Get to the hospital with Molvos as soon as you can." I cut the link and hurried outside to find my dad waiting for me.

"All sorted?"

"They're meeting us there."

He kept glancing at me as we hurried toward the hospital.

"What is it?" I swiped my hand across my chin in case I had pizza cheese smeared on my face.

He shook his head and looked away. "I don't know. You remind me of someone. I wish I knew who it was."

I pressed my lips together. No kidding I reminded him of someone. There was something inside Dad giving him a nudge, trying to remind him of his past and what he left behind.

"You'll figure it out," I said.

"You could just tell me," he said. "I know you're hiding something. You get this weird look in your eyes, as if you're about to share a big secret. You should just spit it out."

"I will when the time is right and we don't have a murder to solve."

"Two murders," he said. "Neither of which were committed by me or Molvos."

"I believe you," I said.

"Huh! It's been a long time since anyone said that to me."

"You're a good man," I said. "You may hide it well, but I can see that."

"You don't know me well enough to say dumb things like that."

"You'd be surprised."

He snorted a laugh. "You're a lousy judge of character."

By the time we reached the hospital, Sophie and Molvos were waiting outside.

Molvos bounced on his toes when he saw Abel and grinned. "I knew you'd come through for me, buddy."

"It's got more to do with her than me." Abel slung a thumb in my direction. "She can't seem to leave these murders alone. Keeps on about justice or some such trash. It makes no sense to me."

"It was a joint effort," I said. "Abel has been fighting your corner, even though he doesn't like to admit it."

"Sophie said something about a shapeshifter." Molvos looked at me. "I can't do that. This is my one and only shape."

"Let's head into the hospital and see Mrs. Winkler," I said. "She could have some interesting answers for us."

Sophie touched my arm as Molvos and Abel walked ahead of us into the hospital. "I'm bending the rules for you. We left the building without all the forms completed. I've got my angels working on them, but if anyone finds out we're doing this without the appropriate authority in place, I could get in trouble."

"If any of this goes wrong, I'll take the blame. We're hunting a killer, and we're so close to catching them. Sometimes, you have to bend the rules to get the bad guy."

"Or in this case, a bad old woman. Mrs. Winkler?" Sophie shook her head. "She's so fragile. Are you certain about this? I can't risk another blemish on the department's record. I may lose my job."

"It won't come to that. Let me do the talking. If this goes wrong, you can blame it all on me. Say I pushed you into it. If I ask the questions, Mrs. Winkler can only support the fact I interrogated her. Your halo will stay unblemished."

"Gentle questioning only, please," Sophie said. "You don't want to make her any sicker than she already is."

"I'll be as gentle as I can." I'd put thumb screws on this old lady if it meant I got the truth out of her.

We checked in at the reception desk to discover which room Mrs. Winkler was in.

"Hey! What are you all doing here?" Bandit strode over, her arms full of vending machine snacks.

"We've had a breakthrough in the case," I said. I gave her a quick debrief about my suspicions about Mrs. Winkler. "Why are you here?"

"Visiting the sweet old lady you now think is a double murderer," Bandit said. "Are you sure about this? She seems nice. She couldn't be less of a killer if she tried."

"Yes! I'm sure. People need to stop asking me that. Come on. It's time to speak to her." I entered the room first and was surprised to see Brendan and Saul there.

Brendan jumped to his feet, his red eyes widening. "Tempest, I'm glad to see you. Your pet fairy has been causing problems."

Bandit lobbed a packet of chips at his head as she entered the room. "I'm no one's pet. And I'm not a problem. I've been entertaining everyone with the stories of my heroic past."

"She got chased out twice by the doctor for messing with the medical equipment," Brendan said, dodging another packet of chips. "And she keeps shedding glitter like it's fur."

"Tell tale," Bandit said. "I'll have those chips back if you keep saying mean things."

"Did you tell them the story about the time you were a ginger cat with an attitude?" I asked.

Bandit glared at me before slumping into the seat Brendan had vacated. "I forgot about that. It's not exciting."

Mrs. Winkler sat in the bed, staring at us all. "My! What a crowd. Are you all here to see me?"

Abel leaned against the wall, glaring at Mrs. Winkler. Molvos stood beside him, shifting from foot to foot.

Sophie cleared her throat and approached the bed. "We need to ask you a few questions if you're feeling up to it." She looked at me and nodded.

"What's going on?" Saul asked. "This looks like official business. Can't you see this is a sick old lady? She doesn't want to be troubled while she's healing."

"Let me be the judge of that," I said. "Mrs. Winkler, do you remember me?"

"Of course. You're the young lady who ran into me," she said. "You're hard to forget. I remember you every time my hip aches."

"I am sorry about that. It was an accident," I said. "I was surprised to see you there. I didn't get a chance to ask what you were doing in that part of town."

"Oh! Just taking a walk," she said. "I often go walking on my own."

"Had you come from any of the stores? Or perhaps you'd been to the house Herbert had rented. Maybe to see Virginia?"

"No, I hadn't been there." She glanced around the group. "Why are you asking me this?"

"I'd like to know that too," Saul said. "Perhaps we should get a lawyer involved."

"I'm interested in your magic ability," I said to Mrs. Winkler.

"My magic isn't up to much these days. It's faded, along with my beauty." She patted her bed sheet. "I don't do much magic these days, anyway. It's tiring. I prefer the simple things in life."

"You don't have the ability to shape shift?" I asked.

Her mouth opened before she snapped it shut. "That would take great power. I'd be exhausted for days if I did such a spell."

"But you could do it?" I asked.

"Maybe fifty years ago." She gave a small laugh. "I have no need for such powerful magic. My son always takes care of me. At least, he used to. I don't know what I'm going to do without him to look out for me."

"You're not alone," Saul said. "We'll make sure you're looked after."

"You could always spend the wealth that'll come your way, thanks to Herbert's new book," I said. "As his living relative, you'll benefit from the fortune he'd have made if he'd lived."

"That's out of order." Saul jumped from his seat. "You sound as if you're accusing Mrs. Winkler of being involved with Herbert's murder."

I smiled at him. "Are you being so nice to her in the hope of getting your hands on all of that money? You want to keep the old lady sweet so she doesn't take the cash and run. Or maybe, take the money and shape shift so you have no clue how to find her."

"I wouldn't steal from an old woman. I've never been so insulted."

"Stick around. I'm just getting started." I turned my attention back to Mrs. Winkler. "What was your relationship like with your son?"

"It was good. He was kind to me," she said. "I don't like your tone, young lady. It's time you left. In fact, you all need to go. I have to rest to make sure the healing spells work."

Saul glared at me. "Why aren't you charging that demon with the murders?" He jabbed a finger at Molvos.

I lifted a hand to stop Molvos from protesting. "He has alibis for both murders."

Mrs. Winkler's hand fluttered against her chest. "You can't trust the word of a demon. They're born liars. That's what my son planned to eradicate. He wanted to give the demon cure to anyone so they could remove this scourge."

"I'm not a scourge," Molvos said.

"Demons have their place," I said. "The cure Herbert was working on wasn't even successful."

"It worked on me," Molvos said. "I feel good."

"Until you stop taking the medication," I said. "You may not feel so chipper then."

Molvos scratched the tip of a claw against his nose and glanced at Abel.

"We need to test your magic," I said to Mrs. Winkler.

Sophie touched my arm and shook her head. "We don't have the authority to insist upon a magic demonstration."

"Let me guess. You need to file half a dozen forms and get them triple signed before we ask someone to do that?"

She nodded. "Pretty much."

"And how long will that take?"

"If we rush it through, we can get it done in twenty-four hours."

In twenty-four hours, Mrs. Winkler would have vanished. She had to be tested now while we were all here. Everyone had to see that she was much more than a frail old lady.

"You killed your son, didn't you?" I stood at the end of her bed.

"I don't feel well. I need a doctor in here," Mrs. Winkler said. "My heart won't stand this stress."

"If you didn't kill him because you wanted his money, was it something to do with his private life? You didn't like his relationship with Virginia," I asked.

"You're suggesting Mrs. Winkler killed them both?" Saul snorted a derisive laugh. "I'm reporting you to your manager."

"Bad luck. I work freelance. If you have a problem with me, you can say it to my face." I arched an eyebrow at Saul. He needed to stop interfering.

He huffed out a breath but didn't say anything more.

"Getting back to the business of murder," I said to Mrs. Winkler, "you were very close to the second crime scene. Why were you really there?"

"That doesn't mean anything," she said.

"Where were you when Herbert was killed?" I asked.

"On a walking vacation."

"And whoever you were walking with can confirm that?"

"I... well, no. I was walking on my own."

"For someone with dodgy hips, it seems odd you'd pick that style of vacation."

"I like to stay active," she said. "It doesn't matter that I can't walk long distances. It keeps me healthy."

"But no one can confirm where you were at the time of your son's murder?"

A flicker of what looked like anger pulsed across Mrs. Winkler's face. "I had no reason to kill him."

"You have no alibi," I said.

"That's not grounds for charging her," Sophie whispered.

"Didn't you say you transported here from your vacation?" I asked Mrs. Winkler. "A transportation spell takes power. You said you don't do much magic anymore."

"This is ridiculous. That was an emergency situation," Saul said. "Mrs. Winkler was desperate. She needed to get here quickly."

"How did she seem when she arrived?" I asked him.

Saul glanced at Brendan. "Well, I can't say that I noticed. I was in a state of shock. She could have been tired."

Brendan shook his head as he chewed on his bottom lip. "She wasn't. I saw her pass the cafe. Mrs. Winkler was almost running. I remember thinking that I wanted to be that fit when I was her age."

"You must have been mistaken." Mrs. Winkler shot a death glare at him. "I never run anywhere. I arrived in Puzzlewood and went to find the angels."

"You're lying," I said. "You weren't on a walking vacation. You used this opportunity to get access to your son and kill him. You snuck into Puzzlewood, maybe in a different form, and waited for your chance to attack. You faked your sudden arrival to give yourself an alibi."

"I did no such thing," she said. "Stop saying these terrible things. I'm not strong enough to shape shift."

"That's another lie. Your shape shifting residue has been found. You were here this whole time. Did you pick out Molvos to be your fall guy as soon as you got here?"

"Hey! That's not fair." Molvos glared at Mrs. Winkler. "Did you do that?"

"Be quiet," Mrs. Winkler said. "You hated Herbert. You're the killer." A spark of magic flickered off the end of her finger.

She was losing control. That was exactly what I needed her to do.

"So you killed him. Then what, you got a taste for it?" I asked. "Or did Virginia do something to anger you? Maybe she found out the truth. She used to date your son, and he told her about your shifting ability. Did she become suspicious of you? Ask a few questions that got you worried?"

"I have nothing to hide." More magic sparked from Mrs. Winkler.

"Or did you shape shift, and she caught you?" I asked. "You had to kill her to keep her quiet?"

Another spark of magic jumped off Mrs. Winkler's finger as she glared at me. "That young lady wasn't right for my son, but that didn't mean I wanted her dead."

"You'd have needed to kill her if she discovered your secret," I said. "Was Virginia going to reveal the truth about you? Maybe she planned to tell Saul or

Jeremiah. That would have meant another death on your hands and even more people to silence."

"Someone call for the doctor. I need more pain medication." Mrs. Winkler waved a hand in the air.

"That's enough," Saul said. "You're upsetting her."

I ignored him. "You shape shifted into Molvos again and killed Virginia. The timing couldn't have been better since he'd just been released by the angels. Did you know that, or did you get a lucky break?"

"Tempest, you've pushed enough," Sophie said quietly. "Maybe you've gotten this wrong. Look at her. She's shaking."

I was looking at her. Very closely. My gaze narrowed as I stood with my hands on my hips. She was guilty.

"Let's take five minutes so everyone can calm down," Saul said. He jabbed a finger at me. "And you need to get your facts in order and stop hassling innocent people."

"My facts are just fine," I said. "But perhaps you're right. We do need a break." I turned, acting as if I was about to leave the room.

As I reached the door, I swung around and fired a lightning spell at Mrs. Winkler.

There were several startled yelps as people jumped out the way of my hot blast of magic.

Mrs. Winkler's eyes widened. She lifted her right arm, and it transformed into a huge leathery looking shield, deflecting my spell away from her chest.

I grinned as I caught her eye and nodded. "Got you."

Chapter 21

Mrs. Winkler lowered her arm, and the leathery shield vanished. Her eyes glinted as her anger honed in on me.

"Did everyone see that?" I looked around the room.

Brendan hid behind Saul, peering over his shoulder at Mrs. Winkler. Molvos and my dad both stared at me, Sophie stood with her hand against her chest, her wings fluttering, and Bandit grinned as she chewed on a fruit twizzle.

"I'll take that as a yes," I said. "Mrs. Winkler is a shapeshifter. She—" The air was punched from my lungs as bony feet collided with my ribs and slammed me into the wall.

My teeth rattled as my head hit concrete. Something sharp pierced either side of my rib cage.

The little old lady in the bed had morphed into a large gray-scaled demon who'd wrapped herself around me and forced me down, pinning me to the floor.

"Stop right there," Sophie said. "Mrs. Winkler, you're under arrest for—" She didn't get to finish her sentence as a jet of black slime shot out of Mrs. Winkler's clawed hand into Sophie's stomach.

Sophie gasped as she was sent flying through the glass window.

"Bandit! Help her," I yelled.

"She's an angel. She has wings," Bandit said. "I'm sure she'll be fine."

"At least check that's true."

She sauntered to the window and looked out, totally unfazed that I was struggling with a shapeshifter. "I see no dead angel out there. She lives to fight another day."

I sucked in a breath as pain lanced up my side. "Keep your claws out of me." I battled with Mrs. Winkler, making sure to keep her newly sharp teeth away from my throat as she snapped and snarled.

This was no weak old lady. This was a powerful shapeshifter determined to get away with a double murder. Maybe even a triple murder if she could do me enough damage.

A quick glance to my right showed my dad and Molvos watching the fight. They looked crouched, ready for action, but neither of them moved.

I was glad they weren't getting involved. I didn't want my dad injured. But there was a tiny tickle of pain inside me. I also wanted him to help. I wanted him to remember how important I was to him and defend me no matter what.

"Tell me why you murdered Herbert and Virginia." I rolled over and pinned Mrs. Winkler to the floor.

She gave a growly, low laugh. "He was mine. No one else could have him."

"You did kill him?" Saul sounded shocked.

"I lost him to that harlot for months." Her words growled out, distorted by her teeth and elongated jaw.

"You killed him because you were jealous of him having a girlfriend?" I ducked as a claw stabbed at my face.

"I needed him, and he turned away from me. He was struck by lust. It was humiliating."

I blasted her with a restraining spell as she bucked underneath me, threatening to get the upper hand. My spell would only hold for a few minutes. Having been away from Willow Tree Falls for almost a week, my magic wasn't at its strongest. I wasn't connected to any magic source to keep me juiced up and powerful, and that left me vulnerable.

"You didn't want Herbert to be happy?" I asked.

"He was my boy," she said. "He should have been looking after me. When he separated from Virginia, I thought that would be the end of it, but she stayed around hoping to win him back. Herbert felt sorry for her and gave her a job. I couldn't risk them getting back together."

"You'd rather he was dead than find someone he could be happy with?" I shook my head.

"What kind of mother does that make you?" Saul said.

"A lonely one," Mrs. Winkler said. "His work had already taken so much of him from me. I couldn't risk losing what was left. I had to make sure I had his full attention."

"Why didn't you talk to Herbert and explain your fears?" I said. "He would have understood."

"I tried. Dozens of times. He saw me as an annoyance. I was becoming a burden as I aged. He even told me that once."

"What made you kill him?" Saul asked.

"I got angry. I wanted Virginia gone. I planned on killing her, but I never got the opportunity."

"It was you lurking around the house the first night they arrived," I said. "You wanted Virginia dead, not Herbert."

Mrs. Winkler growled. "I almost succeeded in getting to her that night. The silly woman screamed, and Herbert blundered in. So I changed my approach. I snuck into the house late one evening and surprised Herbert. I thought he'd be pleased to see me. He wasn't. He told me to go. He said he had to finish up some work and didn't have time for me. I was his mother. He should have made time."

"You got angry because he turned his back on you?" I said.

"I just wanted him to notice me. He was my only child. I loved him, but he was pulling away."

"And you lashed out?" I said.

"There have been times when I haven't seen him for months. And when I did, it would only be for an hour before something work-related took him away. It became worse when he got involved with Virginia. I feared they'd marry, and he'd forget me."

"You do realize that Virginia was involved with Jeremiah?" Saul said.

Mrs. Winkler's head whipped around to him. "You lie."

Saul stepped back and bumped into Brendan, who still cowered behind him. "No. They've kept their relationship secret until recently. Virginia wasn't interested in Herbert anymore."

"Which means, you killed your son for nothing," I said.

Mrs. Winkler closed her eyes for a second. "His work was still his obsession. He was either working or seeing Virginia."

"And you couldn't stand that," I said. "You'd rather see him dead than ignoring you."

Mrs. Winkler growled again, and the threads of my restraining spell weakened.

I looked around the group. "Did everybody get that? We've found the killer."

They all nodded.

"Nice work," Bandit said.

"He shouldn't have ignored me." Mrs. Winkler's right arm got free. She wrapped her clawed fingers around my throat and dug in.

This was one of the few occasions when I wished I had Frank's power back. I could easily go toe to toe with this shapeshifter and come away with only a few cuts and bruises by combining our powers. But with my magic weakened, this fight wouldn't be so simple, and our close contact also restricted the spells I could use.

I fired several repelling spells at Mrs. Winkler, and her grip weakened. After a hard kick to her upper thigh, she let go of my neck with a howl.

I rolled away and stood, sparking magic on my fingers. "Someone get the angels and check where Sophie is. This shape shifting killer needs to be arrested."

Brendan and Saul raced out of the room, jostling to be the first through the door.

I backed toward the window, luring Mrs. Winkler away from my dad.

He watched my every move but had yet to intervene.

"The second I saw you, I had a feeling you'd be trouble." Mrs. Winkler hissed at me. "You poked your nose into business that didn't concern you. I sensed something about you. Something dark lurking inside you. It's not so dissimilar to my current form."

"I'm nothing like you." I circled her slowly, keeping my distance, until she was as far away from my dad as I could get her. "I'd never kill a member of my family."

"You try being ignored and left on your own for months, having no one who cares about you. It's enough to send you crazy. Herbert was a bad son. I told him that. All he did was laugh at me and tell me I was being foolish. He deserved to know what it was like to be unloved. Now he's gone, that's exactly how he'll feel."

"He won't feel anything anymore because you killed him," I said.

She lunged at me. I stepped to the side, striking her with a knockback spell.

She staggered and landed on her hands and knees, her claws scraping along the floor and leaving gouges.

"That's enough," I said. "Everyone heard your confession. It's time to pay for your crimes."

"I'm paying for nothing," she said. "Maybe you're right. I should take my son's fortune and fritter it away. At least I'd get something out of this mess."

"You won't be spending anything once you're inside a prison cell," I said. "Stand up slowly and keep your hands where I can see them."

Mrs. Winkler heaved in several deep breaths before dragging herself to her feet. She glared at me and hissed again.

"That's it. Nice and slow. We don't want any more trouble."

"Bad luck." She flung her hands out, and a wave of pain shot through me.

I doubled over before raising a shield spell.

She blasted it away with another stinging spell that left me dizzy and stumbling before shooting a jet of dark, pulsing slime toward me.

My dad roared and dodged into the spell's path. It slammed into his chest before I could push him out the way.

"Dad! No!"

He threw himself at Mrs. Winkler, taking them both out the smashed window in a tangle of limbs.

My heart felt like it had dropped to my toes and bounced up to my throat in less than a second. "Bandit!"

She was already swooping out the window as I screamed her name.

I raced over and clutched the window frame as I peered into the gloom.

There was a cry and a horrible crunching thud.

My pulse pounded in my head. Please don't let my dad be hurt. I couldn't let him die, not when I'd just found him.

"Tempest, what's going on?" An angel appeared beside me.

I couldn't take my attention from the darkness below. "Mrs. Winkler killed Herbert and Virginia. And she injured Sophie."

"Sophie's okay. She's downstairs," the angel said as she looked around the room. "What happened here? Where's Mrs. Winkler? I'm here to arrest her."

I blinked away tears as I continued to stare into the gloomy night. Where was Bandit? She was fast on the wing. She must have saved my dad.

I couldn't wait any longer. I turned and brushed past the angel before dashing along the corridor. I raced out of the hospital and around the side of the building.

Broken glass from the window was scattered on the ground. Bandit was crouched, her wings extended.

"You got him?" I raced over to her.

She glanced over her shoulder, her expression tight and full of sorrow. "I wasn't fast enough. I grabbed his hand and slowed his fall, but I don't think it was enough."

A cry fell from my lips as I kneeled beside her. Dad lay on top of Mrs. Winkler. Both of them were unconscious.

My hand was shaking as I reached out to touch his face. "Is he..." I couldn't even say the word. He couldn't be dead.

"He's breathing," Bandit said. "Medics are on the way. I think the old lady softened his fall. He landed on top of her when they hit the ground."

My gaze went to Mrs. Winkler. I didn't want her dead either but for an entirely different reason. If she died, she'd get away with her crimes.

"Tempest!" Sophie appeared out of the gloom, one wing bent at a strange angle as she limped toward us. "You're okay."

I wasn't, but I had to hold it together. "I'll live. What about you?"

"Same here," she said.

I looked down at my dad and swallowed, a tear trickling down my cheek.

Sophie looked from me to Abel before stepping aside as the medics arrived.

"Be careful with them," I said as they checked their injuries.

"We'll need to put a guard on Mrs. Winkler's room," Sophie said. "She's a dangerous woman."

"Of course. You do what you need to do. We're only interested in treating the injured." The medic covered them in healing spells.

"How's my... I mean, how's Abel doing?" I asked.

The medic didn't glance up as he continued to work. "It's a long way to fall, but he's in the best place to heal."

With his colleague, they moved them both onto trolleys and hurried away.

I went to follow, but Sophie placed a hand on my arm. "I've got paperwork to fill in. This is going to take some explaining. And after that, we need to talk about a few things."

I nodded. I'd been hiding too much from Sophie. For an angel, I liked her. "We can talk later. Right now, I need to—"

"Tempest?"

My head shot around at the croaky, weak voice calling my name. I raced over to the trolley my dad lay on. I grabbed his hand and wrapped it in both of mine. "Why did you block that spell? I could have handled Mrs. Winkler."

"You were... struggling." His face was a mask of pain as he licked his lips. "She was strong. She wanted to kill you."

"She'd have failed," I said. "You shouldn't have done that."

"I wanted to. You're worth saving."

"So are you." My words came out choked as his grip on my hand slackened.

"We need to keep moving," one of the medics said. "Are you family?"

I nodded, my gaze on my dad's slack face.

"We'll let you know when we've examined him."

I watched as the trolley disappeared into the hospital, my insides a ball of tension.

One of Bandit's large glittery wings wrapped around my shoulders. "He'll make it. He's part of the Crypt witch family. I hear they're as tough as nails."

I nodded, too choked to speak. He'd better make it. I wasn't ready to lose him all over again.

Chapter 22

"You must let me come to Puzzlewood." Aurora's tear-stained face stared at me from the snow globe.

I shook my head as I ran a hand through my hair. It had been three days since Dad had almost died saving me from Mrs. Winkler. During that time, I'd probably had no more than five hours' sleep as I kept a vigil in the hospital waiting for him to wake up.

"There's no point in anyone else being here," I said.

"There's every point." Wiggles' nose appeared in the snow globe, and his hot breath fogged up their image. "We're worried about you. It sounds like Bandit isn't looking after you at all. You should never have taken her with you."

Bandit, who was sitting beside me, gave a loud yawn before wrapping a wing around my shoulder. "Back off, puppy. She's with me now. You're just a distant, smelly memory."

I shrugged her wing off. "Dad's still unconscious. The doctors think he's healing while he sleeps, so the rest is good for him. They're not sure if he'll wake up." He had blacked out after speaking to me. The doctor confirmed he'd taken a blow to the head.

"He will," Aurora said. "He'll get better. The second he does, you let us know. I don't care what you say. I'm coming to see him. And you."

"I will. I promise." I did want Aurora here, but I knew how upset she was. "You haven't said anything to the rest of the family about this, have you?"

"Not yet," she said on a sigh. "Mom's stressed enough as it is. If she discovers Dad's critical in the hospital, it might be too much for her to handle."

"Part of me wishes we'd never told her what was going on," I said.

"Don't say that. I'd have burst by now if I'd have kept this a secret," Aurora said. "I'm glad everyone knows."

"But what if..." I wasn't sure how to say the next bit.

"What if Dad doesn't make it?" Aurora's voice was almost a whisper.

I nodded, my throat tight and my eyes stinging.

"Then at least we found him. We learned what he's been doing all these years."

"But we haven't, not really," I said. "His memory is a mess. Dad remembers nothing about his parents or his childhood. Whoever did this to him, they did a real number on his head. Maybe he's changed too much. Even if he remembers us, what if he doesn't want to come back?"

"Tempest, we're enough for him. He loves us," Aurora said. "He'll get through this. We all will. We just need him back home."

I glanced up and spotted Sophie walking toward me. Her wing was healed, and she was back to her pristine white, perfect self. "I'd better go."

"Contact me the second anything changes," Aurora said.

"And don't you dare forget about me," Wiggles said.

"Not possible," I said.

"She loves you really, puppy," Bandit said.

I ended the communication and handed the snow globe to Bandit just as Sophie stopped in front of the plastic chairs we sat on.

"It looks like you've been here all night again," she said.

"I have," I said. "How are things going with Mrs. Winkler?"

"She's healing. She's been charged with both murders, and we have a guard on her room to make sure she doesn't try to sneak out disguised as someone else. As soon as she's strong enough, she'll be put behind bars." Sophie patted my shoulder. "All other charges have been dropped. We know Molvos and Abel had nothing to do with these unfortunate incidents."

I nodded and gestured to the seat next to me. Sophie sat beside me. "I don't blame you for thinking the worst of them. When I met Molvos, he seemed like the obvious suspect. And then I met Abel, and I could hardly disagree with you about his attitude. He's on a dark path."

Sophie placed a file on her knees and laid her hands on top of it. "About Abel."

I glanced at Bandit and inclined my head toward the vending machine.

She gave another exaggerated yawn and jumped to her feet. "I'll go grab some snacks. Catch you in a few." She strolled away.

I wasn't sure where to begin when it came to my dad. If Sophie had wanted to find out my connection to him, it wouldn't have been hard. She could have contacted Dazielle, and they'd have figured things out between them. I appreciated she was coming to me first.

"Abel Cross is my father," I said.

Sophie's eyebrows rose before she nodded. "You have the same shaped face. I thought it when I saw you together. I wrote it off as coincidence at first, but the way you looked at him, it was as if you were trying to get something out of him."

"That's about right," I said.

"What I don't understand is why he treats you like a stranger."

"Long story short, my dad, whose real name is Artie Crypt, vanished from our lives ten years ago. He walked away one day with nothing but the clothes he wore. We searched for him for a long time with no luck. After a while, we gave up hope of seeing him again."

"Wow! Why did he leave?"

"That's the question everyone wants answered." I leaned my elbows on my knees and rested my chin in my hands. "At the back of my mind, I always had hope that I'd find him. Then I got a clue he was still alive. I've been searching for him ever since."

"And your search brought you to Puzzlewood?"

"Not at first, but I was given a hint he was here. I had to come. The trouble is, now I've found him, he has no memories of me or my family. I don't think he has memories older than ten years. Something happened to make him leave, but I'm not sure what."

"And you want him to remember," Sophie said. "Are you planning on taking him back to Willow Tree Falls?"

"I need him to wake up first," I said. "Then I have to figure out what's blocking his memories. They aren't all gone. He's remembered a few things about me. But he's been busy in his time away from us. It turns out, I have a half-sister."

Her eyes widened. "Of course. Zandra. When he's here, she often visits. She's a cute kid."

I sighed. "I have no clue how I'm going to tell my family about that. I'm not sure my mom will forgive him. I mean, technically he cheated, but he didn't know he was married, so is that even cheating?"

She shook her head. "Your mom never remarried or met someone else? That's a long time to be alone."

"She never even dated," I said. "Mom doesn't talk about Dad much, not anymore, but I get the impression she felt the same as me. She knew he was out there somewhere and something was stopping him from coming home. She didn't want to replace him with anyone else. Not that you could. My dad's one-of-a-kind."

"The man you know is different from Abel Cross?"

"Very different," I said. "Although not as much as I initially thought. My dad always fought injustice. He'd fight to protect other people. And he did it when he protected me from Mrs. Winkler. He could have watched the fight and not gotten involved. He risked his life to save me. That's what my real dad would have done."

"Miss Crypt?" A doctor walked along the corridor. "Abel is awake. He's asking for you."

I jumped to my feet, my heart hammering. I looked down at Sophie.

"I'll need to talk to him about Mrs. Winkler, but you go see him first," she said.

I nodded. "I appreciate that."

"And when you're done, I have a few forms that I need you to sign. We must make sure everything is properly accounted for."

I couldn't help but laugh. "Of course. Whatever you need. And thanks. For an angel, you're pretty decent."

She smiled. "I'm happy to help. Now, go see your dad."

"You won't—"

"I won't say anything to anyone about your family situation. This is a private matter for you to deal with."

I could have hugged her. I turned and hurried along beside the doctor. "How's he doing?"

"He's in a lot of pain. His physical injuries are well on the way to healing. We ran some initial tests once he woke to see if there was any sustained brain injury. I don't think there's permanent damage, but he is confused. It's good you're here. He'll need a familiar face around while he heals. Magic can only do so much when it comes to healing the mind."

"I'll be here for him, whatever he needs," I said. I took a deep breath as I followed the doctor into the private room my dad was in.

Every time I saw him, I tried not to wince. Dad was covered in bruises, one arm was encased in a pulsing shell of magic to heal the broken bones, and his right eye was swollen and partially shut.

"I have someone here to see you," the doctor said. "Just a short visit this time. You need your rest." He nodded at me before leaving the room.

I hurried to the bed, forcing down my urge to cry. "You look terrible."

"Thanks, kid. I feel like I've been run over by a truck a few times. It's not the best feeling in the world. You should have seen me before the healing spells. At least, that's what the Doc told me." His words came out slightly slurred, suggesting the magic coursing through his body was potent.

"I did."

"Ah, yeah, of course. My memory is a bit of a mess." He sighed. "And you? Get out of the fight without getting too bashed up?"

"You don't need to worry about me. I'm all good," I said with a forced sounding brightness.

"Of course, you are," he said.

A few seconds of silence stretched between us. I looked around the pale cream room. I wanted to hold his hand and tell him how stupidly brave he'd been, but I held back.

"I have to ask, why did you save me?"

"Because... I, well, I don't really know." He shifted on his pillows. "How long have I been out?"

"Three days," I said. "You've been unconscious since you hit the ground apart from a few seconds when we spoke."

"I don't remember that. Mrs. Winkler?"

"Under guard and charged with double murder."

"Good. That fall out the window with her wasn't a fun experience," he said. "I don't want a repeat of that any time soon."

"You didn't have to do it the first time around," I said.

"I think I did. I don't know why, but I had to keep you safe."

I rested my hand on top of the back of his uninjured one. "You really don't remember who I am?"

More silence stretched between us. His gaze flickered over my face, lines of pain across his forehead. "No, I don't. I wish I did. I know that's not what you want to hear."

I bit my lip and looked away. After everything we'd gone through, I'd hoped there'd been a shift, and he'd protected me because, deep down, he remembered who I was.

I cleared my throat and looked back at him. "Is there anyone you want me to contact? What about your daughter?"

"No, she'll only panic. Besides, she's with her mom. That's the best place for her. I'll tell her what happened when I'm healed. She'll think it's a great adventure story. Her dad taking out a demon."

"Good idea. You don't want anyone in your family to get upset." I choked on the last word and dropped my head, covering my face with my hair.

"Hey, what's up? I get that tackling a demon sucks, but this wasn't your first time dealing with a soul sucking monster. Don't tell me this one got to you."

I'd held in my frustration and pain for so long, but it was finally cracking through my walls. When I'd had Herbert and Virginia's murders to focus on, I'd been able to hold it together. Not anymore. The hurt oozed out of me, and I couldn't hold back the tears.

"No water works. I never know what to do when a woman starts crying," he said. "If you're upset about the way I look, I've been in worse situations. I always bounce back. I'm hardy like that. I'll have a few scars. That's a good thing. Ladies love the scars."

"You shouldn't even be in here," I forced out. Tears trickled down my cheek and met at the point of my chin. I didn't wipe them away, I let them fall. I'd had enough of holding everything in.

I was devastated my dad didn't remember me. All this searching was for nothing. I'd have to return home and tell my family I'd failed them. I hadn't been able to get Dad to come with me. He didn't remember us. He didn't want us.

"Tempest, kiddo. This isn't like you."

"How would you know what I'm like? You don't know me." It was a childish thing to say, but that's exactly how I felt. I wanted my dad to comfort me and tell me everything was going to be okay, but he never would.

Tears dripped off the end of my chin and landed on the back of his hand.

"I don't want you—" He stiffened in the bed and his body jerked, his chest thrusting upright and his legs going straight.

My head shot up, and I stared at him. "Are you in pain? Shall I get the doctor?"

His eyes rolled back in his head as he continued to jerk, his hand latching onto mine and holding on tight.

"Dad! What is it?"

A gray mist emerged from his body and swirled around him.

My gaze darted about, and I sparked magic on my fingers as I tried to find the source of the mist.

The magic that rolled around us had an ancient, foul smell. It slid over my skin and stung as if it was acidic.

Dad was holding onto my hand so tightly the blood was cut off and my fingertips tingled.

I sucked in a breath to scream for the doctor when a flare of white hot pain flooded up my spine. My head fell back as Frank's energy reared inside me.

"Hey, Tempest. Have you missed me?" Frank asked.

My response was to gurgle as his hot demon energy swirled around me. What was happening? The whole room was tilting, and I couldn't focus.

"Frank?" I gasped out.

"I'm here. I've always been here. It seems you've been messing with things you don't understand. You should have stayed away. You should never have gone looking for your dad."

The flare of pain quietened as the gray mist around my dad evaporated.

I sucked in a breath as the room stop spinning, and Dad's grip on my hand loosened.

He blinked at me, confusion covering his face. "Tempest? Is that you?"

I fought against Frank's energy, which hovered at the edge of my control. It had been months since I'd felt his power. It was stronger and darker than I remembered. "I'm still here. I haven't gone anywhere."

"I don't understand," my dad said. "You look... different. Older."

My eyebrows shot up. "Wait, you know me? You know we're related to each other?"

His head tilted a fraction. "Of course I do. You're my daughter."

Chapter 23

"You should stay." Bandit nudged me so hard that I staggered to the side as we stood outside the hospital. "You still haven't been to the water park with me."

"You can't want to go there again," I said. "You've been three times in the last week."

It had been five days since my dad got his memories back, and some things hadn't changed. Bandit was still behaving like an overgrown child with a dangerous glint in her eyes and a liking for glitter.

"I'm not thinking about me. I'm concerned about your wellbeing. Although, the sonic slide is amazing. Besides, it's a big park. You can never get bored at a water park." Bandit raised an eyebrow as her gaze ran over me. "And you need a vacation. These last couple of weeks have been stressful. Even I've been comfort eating."

"You're as bad as Wiggles when it comes to food," I said. "Any excuse to stuff something down your throat."

"I'm nothing like that stinky hellhound," she said. "But hanging out with you is a stressful business. No wonder Wiggles turns to brownies and doughnuts at every opportunity to cope with you being his owner."

"I'm not that bad." I tugged the ends of my hair. "I just find myself in tricky situations from time to time."

"Two murders." She counted them off on her fingers. "One missing dad found who had no memory. A bumbling group of angels chasing their feathers and not sure what to do next. Believe me, I've never felt stress like it."

"You get used to it," I said. But the last two weeks had been intense, and I was mildly attracted to the idea of cutting loose and jumping on the log flume. A blast in the face with some icy water might clear my muddled thoughts. After the hours I'd spent with my dad in the hospital, catching him up on the last ten years back home, I needed something big to straighten me out.

"I still think you should hang out in Puzzlewood for a bit longer. I've barely seen you. You only come back to the motel to shower and sleep for a few hours. The rest of the time, you've been here."

"Dad needed me around. We had a lot to talk about." That was the understatement of the year.

I still wasn't certain what had happened, but my tears hitting his skin had somehow activated his memories. He still couldn't remember why he left Willow Tree Falls in the first place, but he remembered us all, and that was a great start. The rest would follow.

"You must come have fun with me," Bandit said. "Puzzlewood is a place for families to enjoy themselves."

I arched a brow at her. "We're family now?"

She showered glitter over my head. "Of course. Your sister adopted me. Therefore, you're my auntie. Aren't you the lucky one?"

I shuddered but then smiled at her. Having this crazy fairy on my side wasn't such a bad thing. "So long as I don't have to get you a gift on your birthday."

"Having you in my life is gift enough."

I shook my head, surprisingly pleased at the thought of being a part of Bandit's family. "You could come with us. Aurora would love to see you."

"I miss her, but she's going to have her hands full. You all are." Her gaze turned to the entrance of the hospital.

My dad stood by the door, tugging at the hem of his T-shirt as he adjusted the bag on his shoulder. His physical injuries had healed, thanks to the amazing work of the magic wielding doctors, but his mind was a work in progress.

We were making steps in the right direction, though. And best of all, Dad had agreed to come back with me to Willow Tree Falls to see everyone.

I couldn't decide if I was nervous or terrified by that prospect. It felt like a huge, churning mix of both in my stomach.

Dad walked over, his gaze shifting from me to Bandit.

"Are you good to go?" Nerves made my pulse bounce. What if he'd changed his mind?

"All set," he said, the smile on his face tight. "You're sure this is a good idea?"

I lifted my shoulders. "Honestly, I don't know. I hope so. Everyone wants to see you."

"I should give them more time. It's going to be a big adjustment for all of us."

I touched his arm. "They are happy you're back. Everyone wants you home."

"Home." Dad looked around. "I haven't had a home in a long time."

"You have. You just forgot about it for a while." I tried to sound relaxed, but my heart pounded in my throat. He had to come with me. He couldn't turn his back on us again.

"I bet they've got a thousand questions," he said. "I just hope I can answer them."

"It'll be great to see the old family again." Bandit slapped him on the shoulder. "I love hanging out with the Crypt witches. You've raised two amazing daughters. And your wife's an awesome cook."

"Three daughters," I said quietly. That was a huge minefield we'd yet to tackle. We'd discussed my half-sister, but that was about as far as we'd gotten. I wanted to meet her, but right now, it was one scary, complicated step at a time.

"Tempest, I'm glad I caught you before you left." Sophie hurried toward us, a smile on her face.

"Did I forget to sign a form?" I asked.

She chuckled as she stopped in front of me. "Nothing like that. All the paperwork is in order. I wanted to thank you for your help in solving Herbert and Virginia's murders. I'm not sure what

I'd have done if you hadn't been in Puzzlewood when it all happened."

"Wait a second, you just said the word *murder*," Bandit said. "Did you also hurt your head when you got knocked out the window by Mrs. Winkler?"

Sophie grinned. "I'm shaking things up in Puzzlewood. I'm streamlining the paperwork process, and we're all having training in how to deal with serious crime. We live in an ever-changing world. Bad things happen, and we shouldn't shy away from them or cover them up because they're not pleasant."

"I'd grown to like the way you called a gruesome murder an unfortunate incident. It was quaint," Bandit said.

Sophie winced. "It'll take a while to get things to change around here, but I like the direction we're taking. Thanks again, Tempest."

"You're welcome," I said.

She nodded at my dad, a flicker of caution crossing her face. "I hope things work out for you, Abel. Or should I start calling you Artie from now on?"

He scrubbed a hand across his chin. "I still answer to both, but Artie feels right. I'm Artie Crypt. I remember that much."

Sophie held out a hand, and he shook it. "Well, I'll officially welcome you to Puzzlewood, Artie, and also say goodbye. Have a safe trip home. Enjoy getting to know your family all over again."

His eyes widened as he shook her hand. "Thanks. It's something I never thought I'd need to do, but I am looking forward to it. I'm still trying to get past the fact everyone has aged ten years. I remember Tempest as a teenager with frizzy hair and an attitude."

"Hey! I didn't have an attitude," I said.

"I bet you were an awful teenager," Bandit said. "And you still have an attitude, even though you're all grown up."

I shook my head. "My attitude is just fine."

Bandit turned to my dad. "You've aged too. Don't forget that. It won't be long before you're a silver fox."

My dad grimaced. "I know. But all the memories I have of everyone else are from ten years ago."

"We'll figure it out," I said to him. "Mom's still as pretty as ever."

He let out a sigh. "Yeah, I bet she is. She always was a looker. Smart, pretty, funny. I was a goner the first time we met."

"Well, best of luck." Sophie nodded a final goodbye before walking away.

I rubbed the end of my nose, and my hand came away smeared with blood. I turned my back on everyone and grabbed a tissue out of my pocket.

Ever since Frank had reactivated and my dad had gotten his memories back, I'd been suffering with nosebleeds. It had to be connected. But right now, I was focused on getting Dad home. I'd deal with the Frank issue at a later date. But I couldn't wait too long. Ever since he'd started talking to me again, I'd felt weak. I was hoping a part of that was the stress of everything that had happened and being away from Willow Tree Falls, but I wasn't so sure. I no longer felt in complete control of this demon. And that scared me.

"Is everything okay?" Dad touched my shoulder.

I dabbed my nose before stuffing my tissue back in my pocket. "All good here."

His gaze ran over my face before he looked at the ground. "Are you sure everyone wants me back home? I'll understand if they're hesitant to take me in."

"They all want you back," I said. "Of course, they're nervous about seeing you again and will have lots of questions, but everyone wants you home. It's where you belong."

"I don't want them to be disappointed in me," he said. "I've only told you some of what I've been through in the last decade. Not all of that was great."

"But you weren't yourself," I said, trying to keep the desperation out of my voice. "And we'll figure it out. They'll understand. Aurora practically had to pin Mom down to stop her from coming here when she found out what was going on."

"Cora," he said quietly. "How will she handle the fact I have another child? She'll hate me."

"I wish I could tell you everything will be perfect. All I know for sure is that she loves you. Mom's never stopped loving you."

"At least Zandra now has a big family she can turn to if she needs anything," he said. "She has a flourishing ability. Her mom's not a powerful magic user. She could benefit from being around some strong witches to help her figure out her path."

"I'll welcome meeting her any time," I said.

He pulled me in for a brief hug. "Thanks for finding me. I'm not sure how much longer I could have gone on as Abel Cross. He wasn't a good guy."

I returned his hug, breathing in his familiar scent of citrus cologne. He'd worn the same brand all his life. "He's gone now, and you're back."

He stepped back and gave me a smile. "Yes. And this time, I'm going nowhere."

"Can we get a move on, you two?" Bandit said. "I paid for an all-access pass at the water park this afternoon. I'm not missing out on any of my time there."

"We're going," I said. "Are you sure you don't want to come with us?"

"I'll catch up with you all another time." Bandit scooped me off my feet and planted a large wet kiss on each cheek. "Give Aurora a huge hug from me. I miss that gorgeous blonde. Anytime she wants to go on an adventure, she just has to say the word. I'll come find her. I'll always look out for her, no matter where I am in the world."

I stumbled back as she set me on my feet and turned to my dad, grabbing him up and kissing him despite his protests.

"And you take care of your family," Bandit said as she set him back down. "No more losing your memory and turning into a tough guy, or we'll be having words. Not friendly ones."

"That's what I plan to do," he said. "Now I remember them all, I'm going to make sure it stays that way."

"Have fun." Bandit shot into the sky, sweeping over our heads before heading in the direction of the water park.

I took hold of my dad's hand and squeezed it. "Are you ready to go home?"

He sucked in a deep breath and shook his head. "No, but I want to do this. I've already missed too much in your life and everyone else's. I have a lot to catch up on."

I nodded, my heart thudding with a mixture of happiness and anticipation. "Then what are we waiting for? Let's go home."

About Author

K.E. O'Connor (Karen) is a cozy mystery author living in the beautiful British countryside. She loves all things mystery, animals, and cake. When she's not writing about mysteries, murder, and treats, she volunteers at a local animal sanctuary, reads a ton of books, binge watches mystery series, and dreams about living somewhere warmer.

To stay in touch with the fun mysteries:

Newsletter:
www.subscribepage.com/cozymysteries

Website:
www.keoconnor.com

Facebook:
www.facebook.com/keoconnorauthor

Also By

Luck of the Witch
Hell of a Witch
Revenge of the Witch
Curse of the Witch
Son of a Witch
Framing of the Witch
Trickery of the Witch
Wishes of the Witch
Harmony of the Witch
Remedy of the Witch
Gift of the Witch
Toil of the Witch
Jinxing of the Witch
Craving of the Witch
Union of the Witch
Chaos of the Witch
Sleighing of the Witch

If you enjoyed

Remedy of the Witch

turn the page to read an extract from the next Crypt
Witch Mystery

GIFT OF THE WITCH

Chapter 1

"Tis the season to be a hellhound, fa la la la la la la la la." Wiggles bounced around Cloven Hoof, a string of gold and red tinsel wound around his neck.

"Quit messing with the decorations and help me get the rest of these lights up," I said. "We don't have much time left."

"Christmas Day is ages away," Wiggles said. "I don't know why you're stressing."

"It's four days away," I said, "and we have three parties to deal with before we shut down for the holidays."

He stopped bouncing around and planted his stubby paws on the dance floor. "Only four days? I'd better start looking for presents for everyone."

I finished nailing a large sprig of mistletoe over the front door and climbed down the stepladder. "You haven't got any gifts yet?"

"I know what I'm getting everyone. I just haven't gotten around to buying anything."

"Don't leave it much longer, or the stores may sell out."

"I'm thinking of making everyone a gift this year."

I groaned and shook my head. I grabbed the final box of decorations for the ten foot Christmas tree that sat in the corner of the club and started unpacking them. "Didn't you learn your lesson last time you did that? Not everyone finds chewed sticks appealing."

"Then there's something wrong with them if that's the case. Those sticks were awesome gifts."

"If you're a hellhound."

He trotted over to the tree. "Not only if you're a hellhound. A stick has a dozen uses. You can poke someone with it. Pull something out of a drain. Use it to lever up something heavy. Then you can—"

"Fine. Your stick gift was amazing." I placed silver stars on the tree branches. "Just so you know, I don't want a stick for my Christmas present."

"I'm thinking of getting you some Christmas cheer if you don't start smiling."

"I'm cheerful enough, just busy." I stepped back and turned in a slow circle, admiring the sparkling Christmas lights that covered most of the club. The tree I'd gotten this year was so big it almost touched the ceiling, and there was a stack of wrapped presents underneath it for the staff.

"Tempest, is it okay if I take my break?" Merrie Noble strolled along behind the bar, a bright red Santa hat on her head and some tinsel wrapped around her neck.

"Sure, so long as that drink delivery is unloaded."

"It's all done. And I've got a hot date waiting for me." She gestured over her shoulder.

Axel Shadowsoul stood at the end of the bar, dressed head to toe in black, his dark hair swept off his face. He gave me a wink. "It's looking good in here, Tempest."

"We're just about set for the parties that are booked," I said. "What are you two doing over Christmas?"

"Most likely eating way too much delicious food." Merrie walked back along the bar toward Axel. "Unless we're going to see your parents?"

Axel's dark eyes widened. "Um, my dad doesn't really do Christmas. Besides, he hates the cold. He always heads off somewhere stiflingly hot to cause chaos during this festive time. The Caribbean is a popular winter sun destination for demons."

"Oh, I suppose that makes sense," Merrie said.

"He could always stay home," I said. "I hear Hell is always a balmy thousand degrees."

"Hilarious." Axel shook his head. "Dad's a free roaming demon. You won't find him slumming it in the brimstone beneath our feet."

Axel's dad was a rather terrifying demon, who would no doubt loath the seasonal festivities taking place in Willow Tree Falls. We always pulled out the stops around this time of year, making sure everything sparkled, glittered, and brought a smile to everyone's face.

And although Christmas Day was a big deal, tonight, the longest night of the year, was even more important to the Crypt witches.

"Will I see you both at the cemetery this evening?" I asked.

"We wouldn't miss it," Merrie said. "Will Dottie be making her super-strong punch this year?"

"She always does," I said. "My advice, stick to one glass. Otherwise, you'll be seeing double and might not be able to get out of bed for several days."

"I learned my lesson last year." Axel rubbed his temple. "Your granny sure knows how to party hard. I couldn't keep up with her."

"It's her speciality," I said. That and being an awesomely powerful witch, with a side order of sass and a love of anything sweet.

Merrie wrapped gold tinsel around Axel's neck before kissing his cheek. "We can always have a quiet Christmas, just the two of us. That'll be nice."

"Maybe next year you could have a Christmas wedding." I couldn't resist a gentle tease. "I'll even give you this venue for free if you want somewhere to party afterward. It'll be my wedding present to you."

Merrie's cheeks flushed, while Axel grinned.

"Don't rule it out," he said. "I'm never letting go of this one."

I'd only meant it as a joke. Axel used to be a commitment-phobe before he'd started dating Merrie. This was serious if he wasn't racing out the door at the first mention of marriage.

"We don't want to rush things," Merrie said. "We're happy as we are."

"Maybe we'd be happier if we got married." Axel took hold of her hand and kissed the back of it. "You sure make me happy."

"Get your hands off Merrie." Wiggles stomped over to the bar. "She doesn't even like you that much. She told me so the other day."

"Wiggles! That's a terrible thing to say and not true," Merrie said.

"You said he ate all your chocolate ice cream and then put the empty carton back in the freezer." Wiggles growled at Axel.

"Oh! I'd forgotten about that." Merrie winced. "Well, it's not important in the grand scheme of things."

"My bad." Axel lifted a hand. "I'll get you an extra-large container to make up for it."

"You see, Wiggles, Axel is good to me," Merrie said. "And there'll be no steak for you if you keep trash talking him."

Wiggles' eyes glowed red for a second. "Okay, he's not a terrible half-demon, but I still don't get what you see in him."

"Axel is funny, gorgeous, makes me laugh, takes me to places I've never even thought about visiting, and he's got loads of interesting stories," Merrie said. "What more does a woman need?"

"Not to be dating a half-demon," Wiggles said.

"You can hardly pass judgment on Axel's demon status," Merrie said. "You're a hellhound. You and the demons are connected."

"She's got you there." I knelt and untangled tinsel from Wiggles' neck. "But you're the most awesome hellhound I've ever met," I whispered in his ear.

He wagged his stubby tail and licked my hand. "And don't you forget it."

The main door to the club opened. Aurora and Granny Dottie bustled through, their arms full of wrapped presents.

"We're exhausted." Aurora placed her parcels on the bar before pulling off her red bobble hat and shaking loose her blonde curls. "We've been shopping all morning. We didn't even stop for lunch."

Granny Dottie slumped onto a bar stool after setting down her parcels. "Double lemon shots all around. I need a boost after that. This girl sure knows how to shop."

"I wanted to make sure I got the perfect gift for everyone." Aurora settled on the stool next to Granny Dottie. "And it's all done. Christmas is ready to go."

"Not quite yet." I strolled behind the bar and served up the lemon drops. "We've got tonight to get through."

Granny Dottie dismissed my comment with a wave of her hand before downing a lemon drop. "I've seen enough longest nights in that cemetery to know the demons won't be a problem. Our party will be full of powerful magic users. Those demons wouldn't dare mess with the fun. They know the consequences if they do."

"They can get feisty on a night like this," Aurora said. "I've been cleansing my magic and taking triple shots of a healing magic potion to ensure I'm in peak strength in case I need to battle any demons."

My sister leaned toward white magic, the spells that cured illness, low moods, and generally helped people. She could defend herself against a demon when she had to, but it wasn't something she enjoyed.

Me, on the other hand, I leaned toward the darker side of magic. Not only could I take down a powerful demon, I could swallow them and hold them inside me. Then we had Frank, my least favorite demon, who just happened to reside inside me. He was always a grouch around Christmas, trying to put the bah humbug in everyone's fun.

"Your mom's been cooking up a storm in the kitchen for the last couple of days," Granny Dottie said. "We're in for some treats tonight. Duck, goose, a fat turkey. Then we've got roast potatoes, sprouts in prosecco—"

"Which still won't make them taste nice," Aurora muttered.

"Three kinds of stuffing, yams, sweet potato mash, and all the trimmings," Granny Dottie said. "And I'll make sure to put extra sprouts on your plate, Aurora."

Aurora poked her tongue out. "Don't forget that you're in charge of the dessert." She jabbed a finger at me. "Don't mess it up."

"As if I'd mess up the most important course of a meal," I said. "The pudding will be perfect." It wouldn't be because I was making it, though. I'd secretly enlisted Tilly to deal with the pudding. She'd come up with a triple chocolate, spiced plum pudding brownie recipe that would knock peoples' socks off.

"Auntie Queenie and Mom are bringing the starters," Aurora said. "We're in charge of the mains." Aurora waggled a finger at Granny Dottie.

"And your grandpa can bring anything else," Granny Dottie said. "I've got my punch brewing, and he'll bring along nibbles and extra drinks."

"We'll bring something if you like," Merrie said.

"You just bring yourself and your magic," Granny Dottie said. "We need your energy there to combine with everyone else's and ensure the demons don't forget who's in charge. Willow Tree Falls is a haven for magic users but a cold, miserable place for any demon who puts a foot wrong and winds up in our prison."

"If any demon comes after you, I'll knock them out." Axel kissed Merrie on the cheek.

"With a pot of hair gel and a slimy smile?" Wiggles said.

"Watch it, hound." Axel glared at him. "My good mood will change if you keep that up."

"Do your worst," Wiggles said.

Axel huffed out a breath and then grinned at Merrie. "Whenever I'm with Merrie, I only want to smile. I can't stay angry, no matter how many insults you throw my way, Wiggles."

Wiggles backed away and made a gagging sound, while Merrie giggled and blushed again.

Aurora sighed and picked up her lemon drop. "I wish Lex was a bit more romantic."

"Is there trouble in paradise?" Granny Dottie asked.

"Not really. He's just being slow on the relationship front. We've been dating for ages, and it doesn't seem to be going anywhere."

"Where do you want it to go?" I asked. "The last time things got serious between you and a guy, you got turned into a stone dragon."

Aurora's nose wrinkled. "We don't talk about that. I don't know. We have fun together, but Lex never talks about the future. He lives in that enormous castle all on his own—"

"Apart from his dozens of servants," I said.

"They're his hired staff. They're not his friends," Aurora said. "He's all alone in there."

"He's got plenty of ghosts to keep him company," I said. Lex lived in the recently renovated and extremely haunted Castle Falls.

"You want to marry him?" Granny Dottie asked.

"I'd like to talk about marriage, see where the relationship could go," Aurora said. "Maybe we could go ring shopping, and I'll show him what I'd like in the future. It doesn't mean I want a ring on my finger right away, but a promise would be a start. If Lex doesn't get a move on, I'll have to look elsewhere to find my perfect guy."

"Don't push him away by dropping hints about marriage," I said. "You both need to be ready for such a big commitment."

"Weren't you just pushing marriage onto Merrie and me?" Axel's grin looked wicked.

"That was a joke," I said.

"It was an excellent joke," Axel said. "I approve of marriage all around."

"You see!" Aurora shook her head. "Even Axel can be serious when it comes to marriage."

"Hey! I can be serious about a lot more than that."

"Like what?" I asked.

"I take my grooming regimen seriously." He smoothed a hand over his perfect hair. "And I take pride in my appearance."

"That's the same thing," I said. "Anything else?"

Axel shrugged. "I'm thinking. I'm sure there are more things I'm serious about. Oh, of course, this gorgeous woman by my side."

That earned him another giggle from Merrie. She had it so bad for Axel. I was happy to see the feeling was mutual. Maybe we would see a wedding in Willow Tree Falls before long.

Aurora sighed again. "I should send Lex over to you, Axel. You can give him a few pointers about how to woo me. Maybe I need more excitement in my life. The honeymoon period is definitely over."

"Excitement leads to trouble," I said.

"Says the woman dating the head of the local biker gang," Granny Dottie said. "Don't tell me that you don't enjoy a bit of trouble now and again."

I grinned. "It has its place. And Rhett may lead the gang, but he keeps them in line. There's been no trouble from them for ages."

"Probably because we don't know what they're up to," Axel said. "I don't trust those bikers as far as I can throw them."

"I have the perfect idea," Granny Dottie said. "You two could have a joint wedding."

"Who are you talking about?" I asked.

"You, of course. You and Rhett, and Aurora and Lex could get married at the same time. That would be so romantic."

"Nooooo! I'm not pushing for that from Rhett. We're happy as we are," I said.

"Don't you want more?" Aurora asked. "You've been together much longer than Lex and I have. It's not getting stale, is it?"

"It works," I said. "Nothing is stale. Why change something that's already good?"

"Maybe it could be even better if you got married," Aurora said. "I wouldn't mind living in Lex's enormous castle, but I refuse to move in until he makes a commitment to me."

"Why would you want to go from your gorgeous apartment to a haunted castle?" I asked.

"The ghosts are fine," Aurora said. "They never cause me problems when I'm there. Other than the occasional pinch on the backside when I'm not paying them enough attention, they're really quite sweet."

"That's your trouble. You think everyone is sweet." Granny Dottie shook her head. "I vote for a joint winter wedding for the both of you. That'll see everything right. I love a Christmas wedding."

When Granny Dottie got an idea in her head, she rarely let it go. It was time for a distraction before she got stuck on the path of having me married off to Rhett before the end of the year.

"We still need to get the tree for the party tonight," I said.

"I haven't forgotten," Aurora said. "I had a look at the tree lot Tate is running next to the pizza parlor. He's got some lovely trees this year."

"He'll have sold out if we're not careful," Granny Dottie said. "The best trees always go quickly. We can't get stuck with a wonky tree with wilting branches."

"We'll get a fabulous tree. Tate had a delivery this morning of fifty trees," Aurora said.

"We need a large, sturdy one that will be up to the challenge of dissipating our energy across the cemetery," Granny Dottie said.

I nodded. "We have to get the right tree, or we'll spend tonight fighting the demons and not enjoying the festivities."

Granny Dottie slid from her stool and downed Aurora's leftover lemon drop. "We can't have that. No demon gets to disturb my party."

"Our party," Aurora said. "This event is for the whole village."

"Not just the village," I said. "If we mess up tonight, the demons will get loose, and no one will have a merry Christmas."

Granny Dottie was already striding to the door, all thoughts of winter weddings seemingly forgotten. "Then what are we waiting for?"

I grinned at Aurora. "Nothing, I guess. Let's go tree shopping."

Gift of the Witch is a shorter Christmas novel (around 32,000 words.) It's available in e-book and paperback.